D0408431

Praise For

On These Magic Shores

"Yamile Méndez has woven a magical story about love and determination and the power we all have within. Her beautiful words and Minerva's mighty character, even in the face of unimaginable loss and pain, grasped my heart from the first page. *On These Magic Shores* is equally gorgeous and powerful.

— **Kacen Callender**, author of *Hurricane Child*

"A powerful story about family love, resilience, and blazing new pathways. The magic Minerva finds is the kind that will linger long after you close the book."

— **Cindy Baldwin**, author of *Where the Watermelon Grows*

"A beautifully-written story about hard times, friendship, and the transcendent magic of family. Readers will love Minerva's strength, ambition, and quirky humor, and will cheer for her as she bears huge responsibilities at home, faces challenges at school, and learns how to allow herself to be a kid."

— **Rajani LaRocca**, author of *Midsummer Mayhem*

"On These Magic Shores soars! A rarely seen Argentine American immigrant tale that will swoop in and claim every reader's heart. When her mother goes missing, we fly into the tender tale of one girl's resilience and determination to keep her family together with the help from a friend and the flutter of fairies. A beauty of a book!"

— **Aida Salazar**, author of International Latino Book Award winner *The Moon Within*

On These Magic Shores

On These Magic Shores

Yamile Saied Méndez

Tu Books
An Imprint of LEE & LOW BOOKS Inc.
New York

TU BOOKS, an imprint of LEE & LOW BOOKS Inc.,
95 Madison Avenue, New York, NY 10016
leeandlow.com

Manufactured in the United States of America
Printed on paper from responsible sources

Book design and interior illustrations by Sheila Smallwood
Edited by Stacy Whitman
Typesetting by ElfElm Publishing
Book production by The Kids at Our House
The text is set in Stempel Garamond
10 9 8 7 6 5 4 3 2 1
First Edition

Library of Congress Cataloging-in-Publication Data
Names: Méndez, Yamile Saied, author.
Title: On these magic shores / Yamile Saied Méndez.
Description: First edition. | New York : Tu Books, an imprint of Lee & Low
Books, [2020] | Audience: Ages 8-12. | Audience: Grades 4-6. | Summary:
A friend and some very real fairy magic help twelve-year-old Minnie who
is caring for her younger sisters, hiding that their mother is missing,
and preparing for her school's production of Peter Pan.
Identifiers: LCCN 2019044471 | ISBN 9781643790312 (hardcover) | ISBN
9781643790336 (mobi) | ISBN 9781643790329 (epub)
Subjects: CYAC: Missing persons—Fiction. | Responsibility—Fiction. |
Sisters—Fiction. | Friendship—Fiction. | Theater—Fiction. |
Fairies—Fiction. | Magic—Fiction. | Argentine Americans—Fiction.
Classification: LCC PZ7.1.M4713 On 2020 | DDC [Fic]—dc23
LC record available at https://lccn.loc.gov/2019044471

Para mis hermanos, Damián, María Belén, y Gonzalo Saied, mis primeros amigos y compañeros de aventuras. ¡Los quiero!

And to all older siblings who know what a blessing and burden the littles can be.

"On these magic shores children at play are for ever beaching their coracles. We too have been there; we can still hear the sound of the surf, though we shall land no more."

—J.M. Barrie, *Peter Pan*

Chapter 1

Chasing Shadows

PETER PAN WAS an idiot. Only an idiot would wish to be a child forever. The play *Peter Pan* was for idiots. Practicing for it was for idiots. But if I was going to be Wendy, the only important girl character in the play, I had to practice, even if I sounded like the greatest idiot of all. Twelve years old, and here I was, embarrassing myself in front of my baby sisters.

They both sat quietly watching as I pretended my sister Kota's teddy bear was Peter Pan. But, the bear's beady eyes. The simple smile. The binky with the yellowing silicone. It was too much for me.

"Let's pretend Peter's invisible," I said, tossing the bear aside. "Or let's just talk to his shadow. There's plenty of shadows in this horrible place."

Our moldy basement apartment smelled like a dungeon, and I was the prisoner.

Kota's outraged gasp almost stopped me. Almost. I threw a blanket over the bear to keep it out of sight.

"Minerva Soledad Miranda," she said, her loose top-front tooth flapping in and out, in and out with every breath she took. "Why are you so rude? Our home is not horrible." It was Mamá speaking through my six-year-old sister. "And don't be mean to Mister Browny! He can't breathe!"

I grabbed my hair and silent-shouted, "Don't call me Minerva! It's Minnie. *Minnie*. Understood?" I hissed and my throat hurt like I had shouted for real. I was frustrated, but not dumb. If we made a lot of noise and the neighbor, Mr. Chang, complained, Mamá would be furious.

I stood in front of Kota, relishing the feeling of being two heads taller than someone for once in my life.

She pretended to be unfazed, but her cheeks turned bright red like Mr. Chang's unpicked apples in the backyard. At the first chance she had, Kota skipped away from me. "Don't stare at my tooth," she said. "It doesn't want to fall because the Tooth Fairy's scared of you."

"The Tooth Fairy? Fairies don't exist!" I laughed. No. I *mocked* her, and to make her suffer even more, I added, "Besides, we don't get a Tooth Fairy. Remember, for us it's the Mouse. El Ratón Pérez."

Mamá insisted on us keeping the tradition from Argentina, where she'd grown up. I'd gone along because I hadn't known any better. Once I'd started school though, and the other kids told me a fairy took their teeth and not a mouse, switching to the fairy had been a no-brainer for me. For Kota, who loved fairies with an irrational fervor, choosing a mouse over a fairy was inconceivable.

Kota pressed her hands over her ears, even if it went against Mamá's wishes. "I can't hear you! I can't hear you!"

"That is, if you get anything! You're being terrible," I yelled above her chant.

She heard me after all. Her eyes went all misty and shiny. She snatched the bear from underneath the blanket and hugged it so tight, it would have been strangled if it were a real thing.

Kota was terrified of mice, but her greatest fear was hurting a fairy. Even by accident. Because of Tinker Bell, and the tales about the Peques—the Argentine fairies—our mom told us, my sisters believed that when I said fairies weren't real, one fell dead in Fairyland. Now, they looked away from me, as if I were worse than a dirty rodent. My cheeks burned. I didn't really want Kota and Avi to think I was a fairy killer.

Hands floppy, I clapped and rolled my eyes while I chanted, "I do believe in fairies. I do. I do. Happy now?"

Avi nodded, but Kota remained stubbornly unimpressed. "Anyway, why do you want to be named after a mouse?" she whispered, setting Mister Browny on the bed she and I shared.

Our baby sister Avalon—Avi—watched us like she was waiting for one more clue to tell her if she should cry or not. Had a fairy died after my words or come back to life after my chant?

Stupid fairies.

I stuck out my tongue and tickled Avi. At three years old, she wasn't a baby anymore, but she was still plumpy and soft. Her beautiful lips! Famous women paid money for those lips, and she got them because she won the genetic lottery with her dark skin and her curly blonde hair. She could be a baby model. So unlike me, who as a baby had been so ugly, I'd been almost cute. But not Avi. She was a real beauty.

To run away from me, she hid behind her blanket.

A brown eye peeked through a hole in the flannel, right where Winnie the Pooh's head was supposed to be. Our eyes met, and although she smiled when I tickled and tickled, she didn't make a sound. She never did. She squirmed out of my fingers' reach.

I'd give anything to hear her voice.

Kota put down Mister Browny and held her arms out for Avi. I sat on the bed in front of them, ready to pour out the secrets of my soul to the only people I knew wouldn't go out and spread them everywhere.

"Minerva's a stupid name," I said. "Why couldn't I get a name like yours, Dakota? Or like Avalon?"

"Avalon is the best name of all," Kota said, patting Avi's golden curls. I heard the happiness in her voice because I'd said her name was better than mine.

I nodded. Avalon was lovely. It was the name of the queen of the fairies. The name of an angel, and my baby sister was an angel. The only one I'd ever met.

"McGonagall in Harry Potter is Minerva, you know?"

"Do you think people at school don't say that to me at least a million times a day?" My voice was prickly and harsh. I hated the way it sounded, but I couldn't stop being so mean.

Kota was quiet for a second or two. Then she said, "If you always get in such a bad mood when you practice, why do you even want to be Wendy?"

I glanced away from her dark brown eyes, so dark they looked black. She understood a lot more than a six-year-old should.

"Every single year for the last fifty years or so, the school does the *Peter Pan* play."

"Every year?" Kota asked.

"Every. Year."

She shrugged. "It's about fairies. It's the best story ever, that's why."

She didn't understand anything. "It's not the best! If you listened to Mamá, you'd know it's more than about fairies. Now let me talk, will you?"

Kota and Avi watched me with huge eyes, and I continued, "The kids who get the lead roles in the play get elected as student body president and vice president for the next school year, eighth grade, when school really matters," I said in a singsongy voice. "If one day I'm going to be—"

"The first Latina president of the United States. I know, you say that every day."

I sent her my specialty smile: the shut-your-face. "Will you let me explain?"

Kota did her one-shoulder shrug. Avi nuzzled closer to her.

"As I was saying," I continued, "I have it all figured out. If I get elected student body president in middle school, it will be easier to get elected student body president in high school. And then college. When I'm a lawyer, I'll run for president. Of the country. And when I'm in the White House, I'll be the most powerful woman in the world."

And no one, no one, would tell me what to do.

To Kota's credit, she didn't even bat an eyelash. "Okay then," she said after a couple of heartbeats. "Let's practice a little more. But remember, if you're going to be Wendy, try to sound soft and sweet. That other girl—"

"Bailey Cooper," I said, hating my name even more when I compared it to Bailey's. I'd heard Bailey Cooper telling her friends she'd audition for Wendy, and no one else would dare compete against her. They wouldn't risk losing her friendship. But Wendy's role was mine. *Mine*.

"Yes, Bailey Cooper, the girl on the billboard!" Kota's eyes sparkled in adoration. She clasped her hands under her chin. "Bailey's voice in the farm commercial is so sweet! It must be all that honey she eats. Think about it when you talk to your little brothers. Or eat more honey."

I hated honey, but then, I knew good advice when I heard it. Kota was right. I stood up in front of the girls and struck a pose, with my hand softly waving in the air.

"Johnny and Michael," I said in my best British accent. "Let's help Peter the Dummy find his shadow."

Kota belly-laughed. Avi imitated her, clutching her belly too.

"Peter the stupid," I said, trying to make them laugh again. "Peter the poop-head."

Kota roared in laughter. Not loud enough to cover the sound of the door creaking behind me. It needed oiling again. But that wasn't what made me want to shrivel like a dry leaf though. It was the presence I felt behind me, like a cold breeze on the back of my neck.

I should have noticed the time.

"Why do you use that kind of language in front of your sisters?" Mamá asked. "Why do you use it at all?"

I turned around and saw her as she leaned on the door frame. She looked like she couldn't take one more step, like she was tired of everything. Her jobs, her life, me. Not my sisters. They made her smile. I and everything I ever did or said, on the other hand, always brought the flashing eyes and the downward corners of her mouth.

"Disculpa, Mamá," I said, switching to the family language because I didn't want to *deprive the girls of their cultural heritage* like she always said.

She didn't hear me, though. She was busy listening to Kota tell about her day (in perfect Spanish, of course), and looking at Avi like she wanted to make sure my baby sister was all right.

When Kota moved out of the way, Mamá stepped into the room and looked around. I suddenly saw things from her perspective.

The beds were rumpled. The floor was covered with toys, pillows, and the Cheerios Avi had spilled. Mamá put down a huge plastic bag I hadn't noticed she was holding, picked up Avalon in one arm, and started putting things away.

She didn't need to say anything for us to know she was disappointed. The disappointment pulsed from her.

Kota joined her and I stayed rooted in place, not knowing what to do. If I did nothing, she and

Kota would have to do all the work. If I helped, Mamá would say I was only helping so she wouldn't get mad at me, which in a way was true, but mostly not.

Instead of picking up toys, I made the beds and arranged the cushions on top. Avi wiggled out of Mamá's arms, got on the bed I had just made, and started jumping.

"Are you having fun, Avalon?" Mamá didn't use Avi, like Kota and I did. She never used diminutives. Avi and Mamá smiled at each other with so much love. Maybe one day she would smile at me like that. Maybe when I became the president, she'd be proud in the White House with me. "Say yes, Avalon. Say yes for me, please," Mamá pleaded.

Avi kept jumping. Quietly. Silent like a shadow.

A toilet flushing rumbled from upstairs. Avi stared at the ceiling, and with an angelic smile, she twirled in place as if the sound were some kind of music only she could hear, and not Mr. Chang doing his business.

Kota caught my eye, and I had to swallow a chuckle. Mamá wasn't in the mood for laughing. I knew from experience.

After we picked up the room, Mamá plopped

on the floor, like she hadn't sat in hours and days and years. "I brought you something, hijas. Do you want to see?"

We gathered around her like little chicks surrounding our mama hen. She pulled clothes out of the plastic bag, everything in perfect condition, though they had obviously been used before. A hint of laundry softener tickled my nose.

Kota squealed at the sight of a flannel dress, white like fat-free milk, with a delicate print of snowflakes. She put it on on top of her jeans and T-shirt and twirled. Avi found a pair of boots, the expensive kind with lamb's wool inside. I watched, trying to push down the longing. I wanted something beautiful too, but I didn't dare dream.

Mamá pulled out white long-sleeved shirts for Kota to wear to school, and pajamas for Avi. She then handed me a pair of jeans, a couple of T-shirts, and a red jacket. They were brand-name stuff. I bit my lip not to show my smile. Finally, something that would fit me for school. Classes had started ages ago. We were now in the second week of October, but I wasn't going to complain. Better late than never.

"I have something especially for you, Minerva," Mamá said at the end, handing me a light-blue silk dress. The fabric felt like cool water on my fingers.

Emotion filled me like the sun being born inside my heart. "What's this for?" I asked, avoiding her eyes. If I looked at her for more than three seconds, I'd cry. She hated crying.

Mamá smiled. "This is a special dress for auditions, right? I saw it and thought it would be perfect."

I held the dress softly, like it would be crushed if I hugged it against my chest like I wanted to. "Thank you, Mamá," I whispered.

My mom hadn't been too excited for me to audition. Actually, she hadn't been excited at all. She'd said there were other ways for me to become the president of the United States, that a play in seventh grade didn't matter, especially not *Peter Pan*. How did she know if she hadn't attended middle school in the US to start with?

But I guess she just hated plays, not only *Peter Pan*. Once, our church had performed a version of *Joseph and the Amazing Technicolor Dreamcoat*. They'd adapted it to cowboys who have a party at the end. Joseph and his brothers wore Mexican sombreros with fruits on top, as they did the limbo dance. Mamá had been livid and made us leave before the song was over. Back then, I thought she had overreacted.

Kota had been devastated we didn't get to eat the refreshments at the end, but Mamá didn't care about that. She ranted about how people hold on to wrong ideas just because *that's the way things have always been done.*

That had been the last time we went to church.

This, bringing me a dress, had to be her way of telling me that even if she didn't agree with me, she was on my side no matter what. I hadn't expected it.

Kota looked from Mamá to me, maybe feeling the cloud of unmentionable feelings that had settled over us. After a few seconds of awkward silence, she asked the million-dollar question. "Where did you get all this stuff from?"

Mamá caressed her hair and smiled widely. "That's a secret, Dakota mía."

My sister didn't give in. "Did you buy it? On the Sabbath?"

Mamá stood up and walked toward the kitchen. "Of course not, Dakota. I got it yesterday. It's just that I didn't have a ride home, and it was too heavy for me to walk with it all the way. I left it at the nursing home, so I could bring it to you today."

We might not have gone to church in a long, long time, but we still observed the commandments, and keeping the Sabbath day holy was a big one, although I suspected Mamá insisted on it to keep us out of trouble when she was either working or sleeping.

My sisters tried the new clothes on while I put my treasures away. From the corner of my eye, I saw Mamá's profile. Her black hair was frizzy even when it was pulled in a tight knot on the back of her head, and her brown skin looked ashy. If I were the mom, I'd suggest she put lotion on, but of course I didn't say anything. Mamá was like a stick person drowning in her worn-out jeans and a black T-shirt she'd gotten for free when she volunteered at the school book fair years ago. I'd been in second grade, and Papá was still around. BOOKS SAVE LIVES! the T-shirt read. I tried to think of the last time I saw Mamá wearing something other than free T-shirts, but I couldn't remember.

Later, after Mamá's reminder that the fairies went to sleep at sundown, so we had to as well, I heard her going through last-minute preparations before she left for her job at the nursing home. Sometimes she did a double shift, like today, but she always popped in for a bit to put us in bed and make sure we were okay.

"Did you leave milk for the Peques?" she asked Kota. "Remember, they watch over you when I'm gone."

Peques, short for Pequeños, is what Mamá called the fairies that supposedly had followed her from Argentina. They were her friends, now ours, and they loved it when we left them gifts, like a saucer with milk. Stupid fairies! I covered my head with the pillow to block the lies and the disgusted expression I knew I had on my face. When Mamá left, *I* was in charge. No fairies ever helped me.

The usual tightness in my chest pressed down on me. I hated this feeling, but there was no one else. No fairies watched us. It was just me protecting the girls all night long. Who protected me? I preferred not to ask aloud because I already knew the answer.

Kota rustled in the bed. I held the comforter so she wouldn't pull it off me as she kicked and squirmed. On the other bed, Avi slept like those garden statues of dreaming cherubs, her bottom sticking up in the air, her mouth a perfect pucker.

Mamá finally came back to kiss us goodnight before she headed out. She covered Avi with the Winnie the Pooh blanket. She straightened the covers on Kota's side of the bed, and finally, she knelt on the floor next to me for the last directions of the night.

"Stay in bed, and if Avalon wakes up—"

"Go sleep with her, I know," I cut her off.

She nodded once and exhaled like she was relieved I understood that crucial piece of information. Her breath smelled bad, of un-brushed teeth, although she was so strict about teeth hygiene.

"I'll be home in time to braid your hair for the auditions." She kissed my forehead, her lips lingering against my skin for a second and a heartbeat.

"We'll be okay," I said. "We always are." Secretly, I was relieved she'd remembered about my hair.

She stood and stretched and stretched. She yawned silently, painfully. "Dream with the angels, Minerva," she finally said. "If the shadow of a boy sneaks in, don't take your sisters on an adventure. Wait for me."

I smiled, rolled my eyes at her, and shook my head all at the same time. "Don't worry," I said. "I'll be here."

The door clicked shut, and I fell asleep right away. My dreams were full of music and fairies, sneaking shadows and glitter.

When I woke up, I bolted to a sitting position. Our basement apartment was usually dark even in the middle of the day, but a little light still entered through the small, grimy windows. It was too light for six-thirty in the morning, when Mamá always came back from work and got us ready for the day. She usually took a little nap while we were at school, and then at noon she took Avalon to day care and headed to her day job for a few hours until dinner time.

I slipped out of the bed, noticing golden glitter on my pillow. Maybe when Avi was coloring, she'd accidentally stained the sheets with sparkly markers or something. After all her tossing, Kota had ended up at the foot of the bed. But next to her, glitter like a snail's trail sparkled on the bed covers.

Avi had slept through the night. She was still in the same position I'd seen her in last. She smiled like her dreams were magical.

But where was Mamá?

I ran into the kitchen to check if she was there. The kitchen was empty.

I went back to the bedroom. I peeked into the bathroom.

In our dark basement apartment, there was no trace of Mamá.

"Eight o'clock" flashed on the microwave clock, and for the first time in my life, my mom wasn't home when I woke up.

Chapter 2

Lessons from the Middle

I DEBATED WHETHER OR not to wake Kota. Maybe if I went back to sleep for a few more minutes, Mamá would be here when I woke up, her absence just a nightmare. But my jumbling thoughts wouldn't let me close my eyes. In the end, the need to have someone to help me carry the terrible knowledge that Mamá wasn't home won.

When I told her the news, Kota heard me in silence, squinting her swollen eyes. Finally, she said, "The bus was late." Then she got up, got dressed, and combed her hair. Just the sides though. The back was all sticking out. But she couldn't see it and wouldn't let me help her. She sat at the table, waiting for breakfast and our Mamá.

Avi woke up with a smile, but after looking all

over the apartment, she came back to me, opening her eyes really wide, daring me to read her mind. She spread her hands open, palms up, and shrugged.

"I don't know," I answered her silent questions. "I'm sure she'll show up any minute. Let's change your diaper."

She only wore diapers to bed and day care. The lady there said she couldn't tell when Avi had to go, and that it was easier to change a diaper than to clean the floor. Avi's diaper was dry all day and all night. She also usually had painful infections, for holding it in so long, the doctor said. I knew because Mamá told me everything. Sometimes I thought I was her only friend. So where was she? If she had other plans after work, she would've told me.

"Do you think Mamá's okay?" Kota asked, her face reflecting exactly what I felt but couldn't show.

I finished dressing Avi with an outfit that had been mine and then Kota's but still looked great. "Of course, dummy."

Kota flinched out of her worry. Her eyes narrowed in challenge. "You're so rude! When Mamá comes home I'm gonna tell her you called me names and then you'll be in so much trouble, Minerva Soledad!"

She turned on her heels and joined Avi, who

ignored the Cheerios I served her in a bowl. She played with a stack of blocks instead.

I headed to the bedroom to make the beds. It took me forever to get the comforter straight and even on all sides. Even then, the lines of the plaid were crooked at the foot of the bed. After the clock flashed nine thirty, I gave up trying to get it perfect.

I took my books out of my backpack and started doing homework for the day. Already missing classes so early in the year wasn't the start I had planned. Every year I wanted to be the kid with perfect attendance, but something always happened. We had to move at the last minute, or there wouldn't be money for gas. And today, I couldn't leave my sisters without supervision, even if Mamá was on the way. If something happened to them, I'd never forgive myself.

The morning passed really fast.

"I'm hungry," Kota said, holding Avi's hand.

"Already? You guys just ate." I don't know why the words came out so sharp and cold.

Avi hid behind Kota, who still had that spark of challenge in her eyes, only it was wet with hunger now.

I looked in the cupboards and found a box of macaroni and cheese. It was the regular one, the one for the stovetop. Since last year, when I dropped a teapot of hot water and burned my hand, Mamá didn't let me boil water anymore, but this was an emergency kind of occasion.

"I'm going to cook," I said. "Keep Avi out of the kitchen."

Immediately Avi ran and hugged my leg.

"You don't know how to cook," Kota pointed out.

I tried to pry Avi's fingers open, but she held on so tight I couldn't get her away without hurting her.

"It's okay," I said, sweat already beading on my nose and my upper lip. "Let's see what's in the fridge."

The fridge smelled musty even though it was scrubbed clean. Mamá said it was older than the world. Inside, there wasn't much that could be eaten without cooking it. In an old butter tub, there was some leftover rice pudding. Avi loved that stuff. There was only enough for her. I found two apples and five slices of cheese. Kota and I would eat that.

But when I served her the pudding, Avi shook her head.

"Eat, Avi!" I said, my mouth watering, anticipating the cinnamony treat that for some stupid reason she didn't want.

She shook her head and slid down from the chair. She took my hand, then Kota's, and walked us toward the window.

"What are you doing, baby?" Kota asked.

Avi smiled at both of us and led us on.

"I think she wants to show us something."

We followed our baby sister to the windowsill, where the fairies' milk saucer was empty, and where to my eye-popping surprise, three perfect pink-and-cream cupcakes waited.

"What? What's this?" I choked with the words.

Kota and Avi jumped in place and hugged like they had won the lottery. "The Peques left them! The Peques are real!" Kota chanted.

I opened my mouth to say, "Peques aren't real," but what if a fairy dropped dead outside our window because of my words? I wasn't *that* ungrateful. I may not have been a honey-voiced angel, but I wasn't an ogre either.

But it was my job to be cautious and ask difficult questions. "What if they're poisoned or something?"

My sisters didn't care. Instead of replying, they each snatched a cupcake and went on to savor every crumb. For the first time ever, they didn't have to share.

I didn't know what to do. "Wait!" I shouted. "Who left these cupcakes, really? Think for a second."

They exchanged a look of pity for their unbelieving sister and continued eating. They licked their fingers and smacked their lips in ecstasy, enjoying each bite of the pink and cream confections.

I picked up the remaining cupcake from the windowsill and inspected it. The cupcake liner had no special marks or words or anything. I sniffed at the mound of frosting on top. All I got was a hint of strawberry-vanilla sugar that made my stomach rumble and my mouth water in anticipation.

But I wouldn't eat it. Nothing looked wrong, but I decided to keep mine for later. When Mamá arrived, I would share it with her. I placed it on a plate and put it inside the fridge. My fingers were sticky, and I licked them without thinking. Then I panicked. What if it was poisonous? I counted to ten, but I didn't drop dead or feel sick.

After their cupcakes were gone, my sisters sat facing each other. Kota gathered all the library books about Tinker Bell and friends. She always checked out the same ones, the kind with all the multicultural fairies. Then, she continued her life-long quest of indoctrinating Avi on how fairies are so wonderful and magical. Today she was going overboard, adding even more ridiculous details to the stuff Mamá told us every night.

But as soon as I sat down with a book about Supreme Court Justice Ruth Bader Ginsburg, Avi left Kota talking to herself, and brought me her favorite book to look at: *Peter Pan and Wendy*—the Bible of all things fairy. Someone had donated the book to us for a secret Santa event, and the only thing that saved it from the recycling bin was the beautiful illustrations.

Compared to modern books about Tinker Bell and Neverland, the original story written by J. M. Barrie was impossible to get into. The English was so old-fashioned it seemed like a different language. And one time, when Mamá was reading aloud a section about Peter and the Indians, she'd been appalled at the racism in it. When I'd asked her about it, she'd said a lot of classic stories grown-ups loved were problematic, to say the least. She loved fairies, but not Peter Pan.

But Avi didn't know this. She just loved looking at the pictures. By the end of the first page though, Avi was already lying asleep across my legs. She didn't get sugar rushes like Kota or me. After the cupcake, Kota would be awake—and annoying—for hours.

Kota, who had been a little hurt because Avi had chosen me as a pillow, but of course hadn't complained, sat next to me on the floor. She leaned against me and put her head on my shoulder. I resisted the urge to shrug her off. My sisters looked so small.

"Maybe she had to stay longer at the first job and then had to go straight to the nursing home," Kota whispered, sounding her age for once.

"Why hasn't she called?" I asked.

We looked at the telephone at the same time. But it didn't ring. Of course.

"Wait," I said, "I'm going to look for something. Hold her head like this so she doesn't wake up."

Kota slid her bottom closer and took my place. Avi's hair was so sweaty it curled around her tiny ears. The gold of her earrings played hide and seek with a beam of sun that entered through the window.

Mamá kept her address book inside a drawer in the nightstand. Breaking one of her number-one rules (all her rules were equally important), I opened the drawer, although I could hear her voice in my mind saying, "Never look through my things!"

"Come back home" wasn't one of her rules, but I had counted on it all my life. Since she had broken her part of the agreement, I hoped Mamá wouldn't be upset I'd broken a tiny, stupid rule. This was an emergency. A whiff of lavender and chocolate escaped from the drawer. I rummaged through candy wrappers and an old bar of soap until I found Mamá's book of secrets, a journal with a flowery cover.

I thumbed through the yellowish pages and went over the names of people I didn't know. Only one popped up: Fátima Grant, my grandmother who lived in Argentina. Mamá's mother whom we had never met—hadn't even talked on the phone with because she didn't want anything to do with us, according to our mother.

At the very back of the book was a loose piece of paper. *Peaceful Meadows Senior Center*, it read in the scribbly handwriting I knew was Mamá's.

My heart pounded as I approached the telephone.

"What are you doing?" Kota hissed. "She said, 'don't ever call unless it's an emergency!'"

I dialed the first few digits. "This is an emergency, Kota," I said. "I have to go to my audition. She has to come home."

She opened her mouth to protest, but I looked away from her. Someone was on the line.

"Peaceful Meadows, how may I help you?" a young-sounding woman said. I had the impulse to hang up. What if because of me Mamá got in trouble and they fired her? I pressed the phone against my ear so I wouldn't be tempted to put it down.

"Hello," I said, cringing inside because my voice was squeaky and breathless. "I'm looking for Natalia Grant?" Mamá went by her maiden name. I didn't know why. Maybe it was this mystery that made my words sound like a question.

"Who?" the lady asked.

I cleared my voice. "Natalia Grant."

The sound on the old phone crackled when she replied. It was hard to tell what the lady said.

"Excuse me," I said, "could you repeat that for me?"

"Natalia Grant didn't come to work last night. Who's asking?" Although of course I couldn't see the lady, I felt understanding fall on her. "Wait, are you her little girl?"

Well, I wasn't little, so technically when I said "No," I didn't lie. I hung up the phone, and the echo of her words took a while to reach me, really reach me so I could understand.

"Mamá never made it to work," I said, looking at my sister.

My mouth went dry and a sob threatened to escape

my lips. But seeing that look on Kota—and thinking of little Avi, unaware that the most important person in the world for us had disappeared—I couldn't cry.

Someone had to be strong, and that someone was me. There was no one else.

I swallowed the lump in my throat and squared my shoulders. "But she's okay. You'll see."

"What are we going to do?" Kota asked. She blinked like ten times in five seconds and took a big gulp of breath. "Should we call the police?"

"Are you insane?" I whisper-yelled. "No! She'll come home tonight. What if we call the police and they come just when she walks in and take her away . . . all because we couldn't handle a day on our own? What are we going to do then, huh?" My chest rose and fell fast in agitation. "I know a kid who was sent to foster care once when something happened to his parents and he had no other family to take him. And what about those kids on the news? They're Latinos like us, and once they get separated from their parents, they never see them again. We don't want that. We're going to continue as usual. She'll be home tonight. You'll see."

Kota wiped her eyes but didn't make a sound.

I had to do something. We had to pretend

everything was all right. According to my plans for the day, I'd be heading to my auditions now, so that's what we'd do.

When my mom came back and she found out how great the auditions had gone, she'd be proud of me. And when she found out I'd gotten the Wendy role? Then she'd be so happy she'd take us somewhere to celebrate. Not somewhere fancy—a McDonald's would do.

I picked up the silk dress from the chair where I'd left it the night before and put it on.

"What are you doing?" Kota asked.

"We're going to my auditions."

"But your hair. Mamá was going to braid it."

"Well, she's not here, is she? I'll make it into a knot. And when we come home, you'll see that she'll be back. How happy she'll be that we were so mature and didn't freak out. She might even give us a present."

Kota's eyes lit up. "Like a dog?"

I buttoned the dress. A single line of silvery round buttons ran all the way up the front, except for the second one that was brighter than the others, like it had fallen off, and someone wasn't able to match the new one up with the rest. But at least the buttons were in the front, thank goodness. If they'd been on the back, I'd have been doomed. Kota wasn't good with buttons yet.

I made a knot with my wild, wiry hair. "Ready?" I asked, unfolding the stroller to put Avi in.

"You're going to go like that?" Kota asked.

I took a deep breath to keep myself from yelling at her. The last thing I needed was for Avi to wake up.

"Like what?"

"Nothing. I just thought you might be cold."

"I'm never cold. Now, can you please put your shoes on and hurry? We don't have a lot of time."

She did as I said. Carefully, I placed Avi in the stroller. She didn't even notice.

"Let's go," I said. "Oh! I almost forgot. Let me write a note for Mamá. She'll be worried when she comes home and doesn't find us." I scribbled something on a piece of paper. I almost drew a heart instead of a dot on the i of Minerva, but decided against it. She didn't deserve it.

I pushed the stroller out and looked at the stairs in front of me. I hadn't thought of this obstacle.

"Kota," I said, "you'll have to help me."

Kota didn't even protest. That was the good thing about her. She almost never protested or contradicted

Mamá when she needed help. That's why she and Mamá got along so well.

Avi didn't wake up with the jostling and rattling of the wheels on the steps. By the halfway point, I was sweating like crazy, and a strand of hair that I must have missed when I did the hair knot tickled my nose.

"Do you need some help?" the voice of a man startled me so badly I almost dropped the stroller.

"No," I said at the same time Kota said, "Yes, please."

Ahead of us, blocking the stairs, stood our upstairs neighbor and landlord, Mr. Chang. He was like a wire with limbs. His little mustache seemed drawn on with a Sharpie.

His rubber sandals plopped as he came down the steps that separated us and, in spite of my no, he took the stroller from our hands and carried it up.

"Thank you, Mr. Chang," Kota said.

He didn't smile but his expression softened a little. "You're welcome."

I nodded as a sign of gratitude and pushed the stroller.

"Where's your mother?" he asked.

I kept walking, my ears burning. The sweat dried on my face, but my armpits were dripping.

Kota turned and said, "She's waiting for us at the school, thank you. Have a good day!" She jogged to join me and took hold of the stroller handle.

"Why did you lie?" I asked her.

She was blushing bright red, but looked ahead as she said, "We had to say something, and Mamá said to never ever say she isn't home." She kept her cardigan closed with her little hand. "It would help if you were a little more polite to people, you know," she added.

She was right. But I didn't say anything. I just made a mental note to be more polite as we walked in the direction of the school and my audition.

Chapter 3

The Queen of the Lost Girls

ANDROMEDA JUNIOR HIGH after hours seemed more crowded than a summer festival. Besides students, parents claimed the rooms where several auditions and tryouts were taking place. Everything—from track-and-field to soccer, from robotics to theater—was decided here and now.

"Don't fall behind," I told Kota over my shoulder.

"I'm shy," she said as she jogged to my side to catch up. She clutched the handle of the stroller. Avi slept like she was in a bed of feathers.

"Since when?" I asked. I didn't know if her shyness was contagious or if it was the atmosphere and excitement of the place, but my body seemed to shrink, smaller and smaller, the more people looked at us in the hallways.

"How cute!" one mother said to another, pointing at us. Rude.

The moms standing around looked so fashionable. I fantasized that my mom had pretty painted nails and sparkly necklaces. The thought didn't cheer me up. My sisters and I were an island, a tiny, empty island in an ocean of accomplishment.

The worst part of being a kid is the not knowing. I didn't know where to go. In my plans, I was going to make sure I knew all the details this morning. But with Mamá not showing up and my missing school, things got derailed. I needed to ask for directions, but I didn't see anyone my age or a single face I recognized.

I didn't have a watch, but I was sure we had made it on time. I turned in circles searching for one of the white clocks. On top of a row of lockers I found one. A quarter to four. I still had a few minutes to get in the zone, go over my lines, and maybe even check how I looked.

The auditions would be in the auditorium. I'd only been in there once, for the student assembly. Maybe it was the stress, but I didn't remember where it was. And if I wasted the precious few minutes I had searching for the auditorium, I wouldn't be able to do anything on my list.

Cutting through the crowd ahead of me, I saw a boy with longish light brown hair, the color right in between dirty blond and mousy brown, but with skin as dark as mine. A splattering of freckles covered his tanned face. Earphones dangled from his neck, and a skateboard peeked from under his arm.

I'd seen him on my way to school a few times, and I noticed him because he was one of the only brown kids like me. But even I could tell that the things we had in common stopped at the skin level, literally. He had the kind of clothes that announced money. He didn't seem like a brat, though. Once, we made accidental eye contact in the cafeteria. When the lunch lady asked me something in Spanish, he'd seemed interested, and not in the way that made me feel like I was an alien. We'd never talked to each other, so I didn't know if he spoke Spanish too.

"Hey," I said, putting my arm in front of him to stop him.

He crashed into me anyway and looked right at me, eyes flashing in annoyance. "What are you doing?"

I stepped back, putting my hand over my heart for some stupid reason. "Do you . . . do you know where the auditorium is?"

He sneered at me. "I don't talk to sevies." He turned around and left.

Sevies, as in seventh graders? He didn't talk to seventh graders? As if being a seventh grader was a disease, something to be ashamed of.

I wanted to chase him and give him a piece of my mind, but someone beat me to it. Before the boy turned a corner, one of the fashionable moms took him by the arm and whispered in his ear as they walked away, out of sight. He didn't look happy.

Good, he deserved it.

Someone's hand fell on my shoulder, unfreezing me. If Kota had to go to the bathroom. . . . I whirled around and roared, "What?"

It wasn't Kota. It was one of the stylish ladies. She had beautiful blue eyes and the darkest hair. She reminded me of Snow White. She smiled like a princess too. "Sorry for startling you, but I heard you're looking for the auditorium?"

My eyes prickled with embarrassment. Kota watched me with something I recognized as dread. I would prove her wrong. "Yes, ma'am," I said, remembering Kota's advice.

"It's that way," Snow White said, pointing in the same direction the boy had left. "Do you want me to come with you? I'm headed that way to watch my daughter."

I debated for a second. She was so kind, and she looked at my sisters with so much tenderness, but I had to hurry or I wouldn't make it.

"Thank you, but I have to run," I said.

She smiled. "See you there, then. Good luck."

I took the stroller and dashed ahead, Kota skipping here and there to keep up with me. The stroller didn't give me trouble at all. If anything, it opened up the way for me. People were nice. Either that or they cherished unbruised ankles.

"That lady was so pretty!" Kota said. "She reminds me of—"

"Snow White. I know," I interrupted, fighting with the hallway door to stay open so I could go through with the stroller.

"I wasn't going to say that. I was going to say—"

"Kota, please. Give me a break. I'm stressed. Can't you see?" The stroller's wheel got stuck against the doorjamb. Trying not to wake Avi, I shook the stroller until it broke free. Once inside the auditorium building, I glanced around, looking for a sign of where to go. The hallways were as deserted as the main building had been crowded.

If it hadn't been for the boy with the skateboard, who just exited from some double doors, I would've broken into tears. We locked eyes.

"Jerk," I muttered.

That sneer. I wanted to wipe it off his stupid face.

"Well? Are you coming in or not?" he asked. *Now* he was talking to me, a lowly sevie. I wouldn't give him the satisfaction of trying to make up for his rudeness.

"Let's go, Kota," I said, because she stood staring at the boy like she had never seen one before. Reluctantly, she followed me through the double doors the boy had just exited to an out-of-the-way spot in the back of the auditorium where the girls could wait for me.

"I need to run to the bathroom," I said. "You stay here with Avi. We'll go home straight away."

"You need to fill out a form first," the boy said.

Why was he still around? He'd followed us back into the auditorium. I balled my fists and clenched my teeth without turning to face him.

"He's talking to you," Kota said, pointing at the guy behind me.

I turned around just so that he'd leave me and my sisters alone. His bangs covered his eyes. With a hand inside the back pocket of his gray skinny jeans, he placed his weight on one foot. He was easily two heads taller than I was. "What happened to not *talking to sevies*, huh?"

He puffed up like he was losing his patience. "Listen, even for a seventh grader you look pretty lost. Do yourself a favor. Before going to the bathroom, fill out the form."

He left before I could say anything. The Snow White lady entered the room. Kota smiled brightly at her and waved.

"I'll be right back. Be good, or you'll see when we get home," I warned her, dashing to the stage to fill out a form.

I almost said to behave or I'd tell Mamá, but I didn't want to even think about her. Where was she, and why wasn't she here with me, like the nice lady who came to see her daughter like any regular mom would?

The theater teacher, Mrs. Santos, was giving directions backstage. I took a form from the stack on the piano and filled it out as fast as I could. When I reached the bottom of the paper, I was satisfied that I hadn't messed up anything. I even remembered my mom's birthday. Why would they even need my mom's birthday? I didn't have time to ask.

I turned the page, and on the back, I saw something that cut my resolution into a million pieces. A fifty-dollar fee? For participating? Even without searching my pockets I knew I didn't have any money. Even if we did, Mamá wouldn't let me use it for theater for sure, not when we needed so many other things. Fifty dollars? That would buy us food for a week if we were smart enough with it.

I signed the form anyway, hoping the teacher wouldn't notice I hadn't included a check or anything.

Distracted by worst-case scenarios (telling me in front of everyone that I hadn't paid, or the other kids laughing because I was so poor), I headed to the bathroom, where a group of girls from my grade surrounded Bailey Cooper, the mayor's daughter and the star of Andromeda Junior High. When our school won a best of the state award, a billboard with Bailey's perfect smile appeared the next day on the freeway entrance to our town. She had the brightest, bluest eyes of all. And her dark, shiny hair reminded me of . . .

Snow White.

She looked just like the nice lady who was obviously her mom.

Oh, I should have known. Kota had tried to warn me.

I braced myself and looked in the mirror, ignoring the girls' excited chatter. My bun looked like a bird's nest. In the corner of my eye there was a crusty thing that I brushed away as fast as I could. Sweat stains darkened my dress armpits. Instinctively, I tucked my arms next to my body. Maybe I could borrow Kota's cardigan for the audition to cover up.

"Are you auditioning for Tiger Lily?" the mini Snow White asked. Bailey Cooper's cheerful voice did sound like honey. It reminded me of all that was wrong with me being Wendy. Kota had been right. Again.

The smile I sent her on the mirror could have shattered Arctic ice. "No."

I wanted to do my hair, but there was no way I'd raise my arms and show my sweat stains to her and her friends.

"What are you trying out for, then?" she asked.

Spots for girls in the play were super limited, but so help me, I was not trying out for pirate, lost boy, or mermaid. Tiger Lily was even more ridiculous than Peter Pan and all the Lost Boys combined. She loved Peter. That's all she did. What was her purpose in life? Loving a boy that crows like a rooster? Thank you, but no thank you.

Before I figured out a way to say all this in a non-confrontational tone, one of the girls said, "Bay, it's time to go."

Bailey flicked her hair as she turned to leave, so she didn't see me roll my eyes.

Bay. Give me a break!

But before she left the bathroom, she looked at me over her shoulder. "Good luck."

"Thanks. Same to you," I added without even thinking. As if she needed any luck to steal my spot!

I thought she was going to follow her friends, who kept the door open for her, but no. She stood on the doorway, staring at me like she was studying a bug.

Slowly, she retraced her steps and stood inches from me. "Wait a second," she said, narrowing her eyes. "Are you Natalia's daughter? Are you Minerva?"

My blood went cold and hot so fast I got lightheaded. "What? You know my mom?"

Bailey stretched out her hand and brushed her

fingers against the silk of the dress sleeve. "I used to love this dress. Too bad it got a stain in the skirt and got ruined."

My tongue was stuck to the roof of my mouth.

After a few seconds that stretched forever, I managed to ask, "What? My mom bought it for me."

Bailey shook her head. "My mom gave it to Natalia, our housekeeper."

"The cleaning lady?" one of Bailey's friends asked. "I like her. She's nice."

Another friend said, "Ooh, I love those *pastalitos* she made last week!"

"Pastelitos," I corrected her without thinking.

Housekeeper. Cleaning lady. Pastelitos. She hadn't made those for us in years. She always said they were a lot of work.

"I don't know what you're talking about," I said, crossing my arms.

When Mamá came back home she'd have a lot of explaining to do. Why didn't she ever say she cleaned the mayor's house?

Bailey stretched out her hand and touched the mismatched button, the ivory one. "I recognize this button. Natalia sewed it, but then the skirt got stained. My mom said she could keep it."

Her words were like a freezing curse. I was paralyzed, mind and body.

"C'mon, Bailey," one of the girls said. "It will be Wendy's turn soon."

"Okay," she said to her friend. And before she left, she looked at me and smiled again. "She didn't come to work today. I hope she's okay."

The door closed after her, but not before I noticed Bailey's hairdo: Mamá's signature braided crown. The one she was supposed to do on me.

☀·☀·☀

Bailey shone on stage. Although I was still stunned by our encounter, she captivated me as she went through her lines, sewing Peter's shadow back on. Her audition was a five-minute glance into perfection. When it was my turn, I stepped onstage knowing that I could do this, I had those lines memorized and ready.

I opened my mouth to speak, but the theater teacher and her helpers were chatting and laughing. Bailey was trying the Wendy costume on, as if the part was already hers.

I cleared my throat, and the teacher said, "Go

ahead, hmm . . . Minerva? Is that right?" She chuckled, and then maybe because she realized she was laughing at my name and I knew it, she blushed.

I, for my part, was about to combust. "Oh, Michael and Johnny," I said, but my English accent sounded so phony I wanted the earth to open up and swallow me. The skater boy watched from a seat on the first row, but he didn't laugh.

Before I went on with my lines, a wail pierced the silence, drowning my pathetic words. I looked up to see the older Snow White pacing the back of the auditorium holding Avi. My baby sister was crying with so much terror and sadness that the hairs on my arms matched the ones on my head.

"Whose kid is that?" a girl asked.

My feet itched to run back to my sisters, but this was my chance. My one and only chance to start my journey to the White House.

"Oh, Michael and Johnny—"

"Minnie!" cried a voice I had never heard before but would have recognized all the way to the end of the world.

I jumped off the stage and twisted my ankle. But I didn't care. "I'm sorry. My sister . . . she needs me," I said, passing by the skater boy. I walked out so fast my feet didn't seem to touch the ground.

"Come here, baby," I said, taking her from the older Snow White. "Let's go home," I hissed in Kota's direction.

If Kota had only helped me a little, if Mamá would have been here, like everyone else's moms, none of this would have happened. Kota followed me out of the auditorium, away from the school. Out of the neighborhood. All the way home.

"I'm sorry," Kota said. "You were doing fine. You looked . . . pretty."

"Don't lie." Avi wasn't heavy for a three-year-old, but after two blocks my arms were shaking. "When Mamá comes home, I'll be so mad at her," I said.

"I won't. I'll be happy."

We turned the corner and my breath hitched. The front door light was on. I remembered vividly turning it off to save electricity.

Kota ran ahead, her arms wide open in preparation for the hug she'd give Mamá. "Mamá!" Kota called. "Mamá, we're here."

The image of the stroller inside the auditorium flashed in my brain like those scary faces that suddenly appear on the computer screen when you're watching a video of dancing goats. For a horrible second, I wished Mamá wasn't home so I wouldn't have to tell her I'd left the stroller at the school.

Too late to worry about that now. Mamá would have to be okay if I picked up the stroller tomorrow. It was her fault I had left it.

I counted what-ifs as I went down the steps.

If she hadn't left us so long . . .

If she had been cheering me on like a normal mom would do . . .

If we had a dad who could pick up the slack . . .

If I had an older brother or sister . . .

. . . my life would be so much easier.

I took a deep breath and walked into the apartment.

The note I had left for Mamá still lay on the table. No one had touched it. I searched everywhere. It took me thirty seconds. The apartment was smaller than a handkerchief.

Mamá wasn't home.

Chapter 4

The Truth About Magic

Kota crumpled to the floor and had the first tantrum of her life. Her voice went hoarse after the fifteenth "Mami, ¿dónde estás?" or so. She pounded the floor and kicked with a fury I didn't know she had in her. When I knelt next to her with Avi by my side, I could tell she was slowly coming back to her senses, but that she didn't really know how to stop crying.

Avi patted Kota's head, her lips forming ghosts of words of comfort. At Avi's touch, Kota jerked, but Avi didn't pull her hand away and murmured something I couldn't hear. As soon as Kota spied through a gap underneath her arm and realized it was Avi trying to help, her movements became more controlled until she finally stopped thrashing about.

Still sobbing, she gathered herself up and crouched next to me, her arms wrapped around my neck and her tears soaking my blue silk dress. The tears would stain, but I couldn't push my sister away. Not when I needed that hug maybe more than she did. I wanted nothing else than to cry and call for our mom too, but I didn't have that luxury. As the oldest sister, it was my job to keep it together until things went back to normal.

"Shhh," I said, following Avi's example and patting Kota's shoulder. "It's okay. It's okay."

She hiccupped and tried to talk, but her garbled words became a wail of misery that scared the baby. Avi whimpered as her tears rolled down her face. After a few minutes, Kota lay on the floor, her head on my lap. Her shuddering breaths and hiccupping became more and more sporadic until she sighed and fell asleep.

Exhausted,

terrified,

tired,

hungry.

My sister was all of the above.

After what seemed like hours, I scooted to the side, carefully holding her head so she wouldn't bang it on the floor, and once I was free of her, I covered her with a blanket.

"Minnie, up," Avi said in a voice so sweet even Tinker Bell would be jealous.

"Just a second, Avi," I said. "Help me find Mister Browny." Kota never went to sleep without her teddy bear. I searched for him in the bedroom, but I didn't see him on the bed as usual.

"Minnie, Minnie," Avi kept saying from the kitchen. "Minnie, Minnie."

"Shhh, be quiet," I hissed at her. Immediately, a pang in my chest reminded me that I had wanted to hear her voice all her life, and here I was, already telling her to be quiet on the first day she spoke. "Sorry, baby. Don't wake her up."

"Minnie," Avi insisted. "Browny, Minnie."

I looked at her then. She stood halfway between Kota and me, like she wasn't sure who needed more help, our sleeping sister or me, panicking like a chicken with its head cut off. She pointed to the old sofa and said, "Browny, Minnie."

My gaze followed her pointed finger, and there he was, old Mister Browny.

"Thanks, baby," I said as I took giant strides to get the bear that had been sitting right next to us.

Once Mister Browny was snuggled next to Kota, Avi tugged on my dress and pointed at the fridge. "Milk, Minnie. Peques, Minnie."

All our lives, Mamá had told us stories of the Peques, the fairies that lived in Argentina. Supposedly, they helped those who kept a garden or put out a saucer of milk for them. My sisters were convinced a family of Peques lived in the decrepit flower beds by the front door. As if anything cute and magical would choose an old rose bush and a couple of tangled chrysanthemums as a home, but they believed. Who was I to wipe the innocence from my baby sister's eyes?

With Avi watching my every move, I poured milk in a saucer. Just a little, though. We didn't have much to spare. I wouldn't say that I didn't believe in fairies, but I had never seen one. I was sure the reason the milk vanished every night had a bushy tail and gray eyes: the neighborhood fat cat.

The moon was out even though it wasn't even that dark yet. It twinkled at me when I stepped out to set the saucer next to the door.

"If someone is watching," I said looking out into the creeping night, "now would be the perfect time to help. Please."

Although I counted to ten to give time to whoever wanted to help, nothing happened. Just crickets, literally. There was no flash of light with a fairy godmother, or a shower of sparkles introducing a boy who cackled like a rooster. Nothing more than the darkness of the mountains against the twilight sky, and my baby sister whimpering behind me.

Avi, who'd been sniffling every other second, went silent when I spoke. Maybe she thought I was talking to Mamá, because as soon as I walked back in the house, she broke into the saddest sobs of her life.

"Come here, Avi."

I sat on the bed and rocked her, singing "Bah, Bah, Black Sheep," but she shook her head no, no, no.

"Stop. Stop, Minnie," she said. Her golden fluff hair was all sticking up. Her nose ran like she had the worst cold ever.

"Duérmete mi niña." I sang Mamá's lullaby.

It worked like a charm. Avi hiccupped, trying to calm herself, choking me with her little arms. Every time I stopped singing to swallow or clear my throat, she threatened to start with her sadness all over again.

Keeping the same tune, I sang, "Tengo mucha hambre. Let's find something to eat."

I really was hungry and wanted something to eat, but she laughed, a sound so sweet and pure, my eyes filled with tears. I made up another silly phrase, and she giggled.

If fairies were born of the sound of a child's first laughter, how many fairies had been born at the sound of my sister's? I hoped, really hoped, that they would make us a miracle and send us our mother. I didn't ask for more.

"One day," I said to Avi. "One day when I'm all grown and free, you'll say, 'Tell me the story of the day I learned how to speak and the day I learned how to giggle.' I'll tell you the whole thing, and we'll laugh and laugh."

She nodded like she understood every word.

"Minnie," she said. "My Minnie."

My insides melted and squirmed like molten chocolate cake in my tummy. I felt bad for having a favorite. I mean, Kota was awesome sometimes. She was a good helper and a good listener. She was my cheerleader. But Avi. Oh, Avi! She knew me. And she loved me no matter what.

I was about to set her down to find something to eat when someone knocked on the door.

Avi looked at me with her green eyes round as the

full moon. Her features were delicate and refined, like she could be a model baby in a catalog.

"Girls, are you there?" a lady asked. I thought I recognized her voice from the phone.

She clapped her hands. "Girls!"

I stood frozen at the sound of footsteps going back up the stairs. I took a step in the direction of the window. It was so small and so low in the ground, no one could see in, but I saw a pair of white shoes, the kind Mamá wore at the senior center. The woman stood on the grass as she walked back and forth, back and forth from the lawn to the building door like she couldn't make up her mind to leave. Finally, she walked back to the yellow car parked by the curb and drove away.

When I turned back to Avi, she had fallen asleep on the floor, her little hands pillowing her head. I covered her with her blanket and let her sleep on the carpet, not far from where Kota slept too.

Mamá liked to mix her glittery fairy tales with horror stories. She warned us against La Llorona, the ghost of a sad woman who went looking for her lost kids in the night. Once, when we still went to church, a girl from Mexico told me she was going to dress up as La Llorona for Halloween, so

I thought it wasn't a story my mom had made up or brought from Argentina. Mamá also told us stories about el Cuco, a boogeyman that took disobedient children away. That one made me scared of the dark because if there really was a monster that took away disobedient daughters, then I had to be at the top of its list.

More than anything, Mamá had told us time and again not to ever let anyone in when she wasn't home, but I had a nagging feeling that maybe I should have opened the door. Maybe the lady could have helped us. But on the other hand, what if I opened the door and because of me, my sisters were stolen or something worse happened?

No, it was best to follow the rules. I had broken them today by going to the auditions, and I hadn't even had the chance to say my lines. Nothing good came from breaking rules. No, it was right to pretend we weren't home when the lady knocked on the door.

My stomach growled, interrupting my internal struggle, and reminding me I hadn't eaten any dinner. Mamá usually went grocery shopping on Tuesday, and this Monday night, we were out of almost everything. I scoured the drawers looking for spare change, or anything that would help us survive until we could buy food again.

I came up with three dimes and five quarters. Not even enough for a loaf of bread. I opened the chifforobe, as Mamá called an old armoire she'd bought at a garage sale. I searched in the pockets of Mamá's jacket. A wrinkled five-dollar bill lay tucked in a corner, and after tugging a little, it came free. I held it up like I had found a treasure. But when I caught a peek of the corner of a leather wallet, Mamá's wallet, on the floor of the armoire, my heart drummed like the galloping of an out-of-control horse. I snatched it, afraid it would disappear if I wasn't fast enough.

The leather was cool in my hands, well-worn and smooth like Mamá's hands never were. Strangest of all, a thin layer of gold glitter covered it in patches. I wondered, whose? With a stab of jealousy, I thought, *From Bailey's house. We've never owned this expensive kind of glitter.*

I opened the wallet to see if maybe she had bought a new one and had left this one on purpose. Inside, I found fifteen twenty-dollar bills—three hundred dollars, more money than I'd ever seen at once in my life. I put it back inside, behind her driver's license, although she hadn't driven in months, not since she sold the car last winter. One of the reasons we moved to this basement was because the bus stop was only three blocks away.

I wondered if maybe there was a bus strike, like the ones that happened in Argentina all the time, according to the news and Mamá's stories of when she was young. But no, even with no transportation, Mamá would come back to us. Even if she had to walk all the way from downtown Salt Lake.

If it took an hour by car, how long would it be on foot?

Behind the driver's license, so tightly tucked in I had a hard time pulling it out, was a picture of my father, Gustavo. He wore a yellow-and-blue soccer uniform. His long hair couldn't quite hide the smile on his face as he kicked the ball. I wondered if Mamá had kept this photo because he was smiling, or because it was the shot of an important goal, or if it was because he looked so handsome. My skin was the exact shade of dark brown as his. I could also see Kota in his straight hair. His beautiful hair, Mamá called it. I had no idea where mine, wiry and coarse, came from.

One thing was sure though, there was no trace

of Avalon hidden in him. Papá left six years ago. Avi was only three. The numbers didn't add up, or match, or whatever. I thought about this all the time. Especially when I looked and looked at her and saw how beautiful and different from the rest of us she was. Mamá, Kota, and I were like the same person in different sizes.

When I turned to leave the room, I stumbled on the long dress, which I was still wearing. Carefully, I took it off and put it inside the chifforobe. Now that I knew it had been Bailey's, I'd never wear it again. I didn't want her leftovers. Besides, my black sweats and my old Hello Kitty T-shirt were more comfortable than the dress would ever be. Mamá had bought those. I knew that for a fact because I had been there at Wal-Mart when she got them for me.

Once in my familiar clothes, I went back to the living room and turned the TV on so quietly it was almost on mute. With my father's picture in hand, I snuggled in a corner of the sofa, buried under a pile of baby blankets.

The TV reported nothing about a bus driver strike, or about a woman walking through the mountains to get home to her girls. Infomercial after infomercial clicked by, but none suggested how to find lost parents or how to take care of little sisters and still attend school. In the end, I settled on a soccer game from a B team somewhere in Central America. I wouldn't even say it aloud, but in the silence of the night, I couldn't deny that I looked for him, Papá. Sometimes I hoped I'd find him playing a game or cheering in a stadium. Had Mamá gone looking for him?

Maybe she had.

I jumped out of the chair, went back to the bedroom, and looked inside the treasure box in her nightstand where she kept all the important papers: birth certificates, vaccine records, and passports. But Mamá's documents were there. She couldn't have gone looking for him without them.

But what if the police thought she was undocumented and took her away? Besides a piece of paper that showed she'd been born here, in America, nothing else said that she belonged here.

No, I couldn't think of that.

I kept rummaging through the box. In a Ziplock bag with my name written in permanent marker, a collection of baby teeth all but screamed at me that there was no such thing as fairies or Peques or magic. Of course, I'd known for a long, long time that Mamá was the Tooth Fairy, Ratón Pérez, Papá Noel, and the Three Kings all combined. Multipurpose Mamá. Still, my tiny ivory teeth were the proof I wished I'd never found.

In a daze, I went back to the living room and turned the TV off. I just looked out the window, hoping to see Mamá walking home.

Chapter 5

The Shadowless Boy

I THOUGHT ABOUT OUR situation pretty much all night. Waiting at home for Mamá to come back wouldn't do us any good. If I missed any more school, the office might call. The last thing I wanted was to involve grown-ups in our mess.

When the clock struck seven, I shook my sleeping sister softly. "Kota, wake up," I said. "We need to go to school. Wake up."

As soon as Kota opened her eyes, she was wide awake. She wiped a hand over her mouth and asked, "Is Mamá here?"

I hated to turn off the sparkle in her eyes, but I wasn't going to lie. "No. She isn't back, but we have to act like normal, or she'll get in trouble with the police."

Her loose tooth hung on by just a string. Any

moment, it would fall out. "Do you want me to pull it out?"

"No," she exclaimed, jumping out of my reach. "I want to give my body time to go through its natural course."

"Ha! You don't want it to fall out because you're scared the Tooth Fairy won't come if Mamá isn't here."

Pudgy Kota blushing bright red looked more like an apple than ever.

"The Tooth Fairy will come, you'll see," I reassured her as she dressed for school. This lie, surprisingly, came naturally to my lips. The baggie full of baby teeth in Mamá's nightstand flashed in my mind, and although it would be better for my sister to learn the truth—or the lies—about magic and fairies, I didn't have the heart to smash her innocence.

Quietly, like shadows so the baby wouldn't wake up, Kota and I went through the motions of school preparation. I've heard Mamá say there were ten kids under the age of four at Avi's day care, and most times she didn't even take a nap. She needed peace and quiet and all the sleep she could get.

"What are we doing with Avi?" Kota put on her backpack and waited by the front door.

"We'll leave her at the day care. I know she doesn't usually go until noon, but the place is open. We'll say it's just for today," I said with such authority.

Kota didn't complain. She did half-roll her eyes, out of principle.

Avi didn't stir as I checked her diaper (it was dry) and changed her pajamas for a flower-printed dress and solid pink leggings. I didn't do her hair because the cloud of golden curls around her face was perfect.

"Ready?" Kota asked, taking hold of the door knob.

I nodded, my arms full of sleeping baby, and followed her outside.

The air was crisp and sweet like the apples still hanging from the trees in Mr. Chang's orchard. I made a mental note to pick a few on our way back from school. We had the three hundred dollars I had found in Mamá's wallet. I had left two hundred in the chifforobe, and had put five twenties in my backpack. We needed food. Whenever I had a minute, I'd get milk and bread at the gas station. I'd save the rest, managing with as little money as possible. Maybe I could pay the audition fee. Although I was sure I hadn't been cast as Wendy, I didn't want to owe the school any money. I already got free lunch.

"What are you thinking?" Kota grabbed hold of the crook of my elbow, like she did with Mamá.

I licked my lips, thinking with longing of the Chapstick I'd left at home.

Before I could answer, she asked again, "Are you thinking of her?"

"Yes."

"I wonder if something happened to her. What if she got mom-napped? What if she's waiting for us to come and rescue her?"

We were almost at the day care, a small yellow-painted house with a few plastic slides and a teeter-totter out front. I had never seen any kids actually playing outside.

Kota continued, "We can't just pretend nothing happened, you know?"

I stopped so she could look at me when I spoke. Her cheeks were chapped.

"Kota," I said, "Mamá will always come back to us—"

"Papá left," she said, lifting her chin defiantly.

I didn't need the reminder. "Papá's different. They'd been having issues for a while. But Mamá? She'd never leave us." The truth of my words burned inside me. I felt like the religious people giving testimony at church, claiming they "knew" something for which they had no proof. Mamá wasn't here, but she'd showed time and again that she loved us, and a mother who loves her kids doesn't just walk out on them and disappear from their lives.

"She normally wouldn't," Kota added. "But what if something bad happened to her?"

In the time it took me to blink it away, I saw our future stretched ahead of us: the three of us placed in foster care with different people. My sisters forgetting all about me. My sisters getting hurt.

This was the second day without our mother. How long could we hold on without her?

I knocked on the day care door. A baby cried inside.

In that moment, Avi woke up. The whole sky fit into her terrified eyes. "Minnie," she said in that pure voice that did something powerful in my heart.

"It's okay, baby," I whispered. "I need to go to school. I'll pick you up after."

Kota smiled and caressed the blonde curls of our baby sister. A thin lady who looked like she hadn't slept in forever opened the door. At the sight of her, Avi mouthed, "Minnie," but no sound came out of her lips.

The hairs on my arms stood stiff like pins.

"There you are. It's kind of early, but oh well," the lady said. I knew her, Mirta. She was from Argentina too. "Why didn't your mom bring her yesterday? Was she sick?" Mirta had a voice like the tongue of a cat.

"No, she's never sick," I said because it was the honest truth and I needed to pad the lie that followed. "We had company."

Kota's face went bright red, but she didn't open her mouth to call me out on my lie. Her silence encouraged me.

The lady moved her head, halfway between a nod and a shake. "Look at that!" she exclaimed. "Well, tell your mother I want to talk to her. Is she picking up the girl?"

My nostrils flared. If I had super powers or magic, I'd turn this woman into the toad she was at heart. "She won't be picking up Avalon today. I'll stop by after school."

Mirta squinted her eyes. "What time?"

I calculated super fast. Usually Mamá picked up Avalon at the same time the bell rang. If I cut the last class, I'd be able to get here at the same time Mamá always did.

"Three-thirty. Like always," I said.

Mirta opened the door wider. Inside, a baby in a high chair watched *PJ Masks*. I pictured my sweet Avi sitting in a high chair in front of the TV all day. She didn't deserve this. She deserved to be at home, or at the very least, in a day care with someone who was nice and really cared. I didn't want to leave her there, but what else could I do?

"Te quiero, Avi," I said and kissed her cheek, hoping the kiss would last her until we saw each other again.

Avi, resigned to her fate, hugged me tightly and then smiled at Kota. But it was a small, lightless smile. I put her down and she walked of her own free will inside the day care.

Without another word, Mirta shut the door in our faces. Kota and I stood there, rooted, for a second or two.

Maybe my teachers wouldn't notice if a three-year-old attended class with me.

"It's not like the kids in my class can color any better than her. If you saw some of the pictures Bree turns in . . ." Kota said. She'd obviously been thinking the same thing as me.

We walked hand in hand until we arrived at her

school, which was right across the street from the middle school soccer fields. The usual group of soccer fanatics already dotted the grass. No one was allowed to play before school, but the kids just stood there, like they needed to feel the energy from the field or something.

"See you later," I said.

Kota smiled at me and waited in the corner for the crossing guard to give her the go-ahead. In the crosswalk, she found a friend. As if she'd left all her worries on my side of the street, Kota chatted with the other kids like we weren't orphans, as if we were just like the rest of them. Maybe she was. Maybe my sister was the normal one after all.

As I stood on the sidewalk staring at my sister, the guy on the skateboard passed right in front of me. He couldn't go behind me. No, he had to disturb my morning and make me notice him. But the swoosh of the wheels on the sidewalk made me wish for something that would let me fly past people, zig-zag between them. Go fast, fast, and never stop until I reached the stars.

Just as my imagination was taking me to a Neverland where skateboards soared through the air, the guy stopped a few feet from me.

"You never came back to finish your audition."
He looked at me like I had killed his favorite pet.

I didn't have a skateboard, but it wasn't like I couldn't amble around him either. "What happened to 'I don't talk to sevies'?" I'd never let him forget his words.

His face went all the shades of red, but he had a tiny smile that his longish hair didn't cover all the way. "I'm sorry, okay? I was wrong."

"But your mom had to shake you for you to understand, right?" I tapped my foot, channeling the best impersonation of my mother I'd ever performed.

"Like I said, I was wrong. I just wanted to tell you that the theater teacher asked about you when you didn't come back."

"Mrs. Santos?" I didn't want to let him off the hook so easily, but this was great news. Mrs. Santos had asked about me! But what could this mean? Only good news, I imagined.

In spite of my resolve not to let my hopes soar, they flew of their own accord. In a millisecond, my imagination took me to Broadway—one day I could play Angelica in *Hamilton*, or Vanessa from *In the Heights*. I'd never seen either, but I'd heard the soundtracks, and oh! They were fantastic, which didn't surprise me, because their creator and I shared a last name. Maybe we were even related, who knew? In any case, one day, I'd tour around the world, and then, I'd run for president of the US.

"What did she want?" I asked, pushing the crazy fantasies aside.

The guy made a cool move with his foot and the skateboard flew to his hands. He tucked it underneath his arm. "Nothing, but last night after you ran away, she kept asking about you. She looked worried when you didn't come back."

Mrs. Santos had been asking about me. She knew my name. She wanted me in the play maybe because she wanted me to be Wendy. That meant I'd been totally believable as the protector of Michael and . . . and . . . what-was-the-other's-name?

This meant I had to pay the fee before she changed her mind. I wanted to be in the play more than ever. It looked like my plan to the White House continued without a hitch.

First, I had to drop this guy who didn't leave me alone. I went around him in the direction of the school.

Unfazed, he walked beside me. Never in all my years as a student had I walked beside anyone who wasn't my mom or my sister. I didn't know what to say, or what speed to walk. Should I jog to try and match his longer strides, or should I hold my pace and make him slow down for me? But what if he walked away instead of waiting?

"Your name's Minerva, right? Like—"

"Like McGonagall from Harry Potter, I know. Haha. How funny." I refused to even look at him.

"I was going to say like the goddess, but whatever."

Awkward. "I go by Minnie, though," I said.

He chuckled. "Like the mouse?"

I didn't even reply. The faster I got away from him the better. I cut through the grass to cross into the holy ground of school. He followed me, the skateboard still tucked under his arm. "Minnie Mouse is my sister's favorite character. That's why I said that . . ."

Now he was the one not knowing what to say.

I didn't want to make the situation easier for him, but he had sisters. Finally, something we had in common. "You have sisters? How many?"

He chuckled again. "Six. Six older sisters."

I smiled in spite of myself. How cool would it be to have so many older siblings, so many people to take the load should your parents go missing?

"What's your name?" I asked as the bell rang.

"Maverick," he said, winking. The fool actually winked. At me. "My name's Maverick."

The sun came out of a cloud just as Maverick jumped on his skateboard and rode to the school doors. Against all the rules. He flicked the skateboard and grabbed it in the air, turned, and saluted me. No shadow followed behind him.

Chapter 6

Literally

I COULDN'T PAY MY fee before first period because the bell rang as I was walking in the school's front door. Maverick and his stupid conversation had made me late. I had to run to math.

The office lady wasn't happy I stopped by to pay the theater fee between Civics and English, but I didn't want to wait any longer to pay what I owed.

"Mr. Beck is very strict about students being tardy," she said in a singsongy voice of doom.

Mr. Beck and his obsession with punctuality were the least of my problems. English was my easiest class. I always answered what he wanted to hear, and if the year continued as it had, I would get an A faster than a sneeze. I could afford a tardy without a problem.

What I couldn't afford was not getting the part of Wendy because I hadn't paid the audition fee. On the other hand, I couldn't afford the audition fee either, but when Mamá came back, she'd feel so guilty for leaving us that she wouldn't mind I'd used the money for the play. It was for school, after all, and she always said nothing was more important than school.

It turned out the office lady had been right. Mr. Beck took my tardy slip with the same contempt as if I had spat on his face.

"It shows your disrespect, Miranda. When you're late, it shows that you don't care. Literally."

Thank you very much, Mr. Beck. That was exactly what I needed to hear.

If being late meant a person didn't care, what about when a person just walked out and never came back? At least Papá had left after a fight with Mamá. But why would *she* leave us? I hadn't even talked back at her. Not that much anyway.

I could take hours of numbing schooling, but Avi was stuck with the evil witch in the haunted day care. What had she done?

Why had Mamá left her?

Thinking too much can give a person a headache.

Images of Avi and the reasons my mom had decided to vanish bounced in my head like astronauts in space.

Boing!

Boing!

Boing!

My head throbbed. When Mr. Beck asked me what the theme of *The Little Prince* was, the words calcified behind my teeth. A sound that should have belonged to a zombie and not the future president of the Unites States came out of my mouth. I couldn't blame the rest of the class for laughing at me. I would have laughed too if I'd been in a better mood.

But thinking too much can make a person ultra-grumpy. Maybe that's why Mamá always had that frown on her face after a long day of work.

What wasn't funny was Mr. Beck's headshaking and *tsk-tsk*ing, as if I'd let him down. Again. "The theme of *The Little Prince*," he said, "is that the most important things aren't visible. Literally. Take note."

I knew that. He was the one who needed to take note. As my English *and* homeroom teacher, how could he not see that I wasn't my normal question-answering self? That, added to my throbbing head, plus a pain in the middle of my chest, as if I had a swollen stone that grew with each passing hour that I didn't know where my mother was.

"When not even Minerva Miranda knows the answer," Mr. Beck said. "That means it's time for . . ."

The whole class held its breath.

"Pop quiz! Five questions on *The Little Prince*."

A wave of hatred rippled my way. "Thank you for ruining my life," said a mousy kid I'd never noticed before. He had the biggest glasses I'd ever seen on a kid my age. I'd always wanted glasses, but I had perfect vision.

Other people echoed the mousy kid's thoughts, but I was used to putting my I-don't-care mask on. I wore it when Mr. Beck passed out the quiz print-outs (which proved this wasn't a pop quiz, but that it had been planned, and he had used me as a tool). The mask also stayed put while I answered the whole thing in less than five minutes, although I'd used complete sentences and examples.

While the rest of the class scrambled to answer what the rose meant (universal love) and the symbolism behind the snake bite (returning home), I looked around me, noticing things and people I'd never noticed before.

The guy on my right, Ravi, caught my eye and

mouthed, "It's all your fault!" His dad was a rich doctor who ran a clinic for the poor. Mamá had taken me there for a middle school physical exam. I felt guilty that I couldn't return the kindness. I didn't like owing things to people. So when he stretched his neck to peek onto my paper, I let him copy my answer. My intellectual property was all I could share.

A girl and a boy who I thought were related, if not straight out brother and sister, didn't try to copy or to even pretend they were working on the quiz. They had brown skin like mine, maybe a little lighter. They looked as lost as I had felt the day of the audition, looking for the auditorium.

The way they lowered their eyes when the teacher walked past their desks, the way the teacher never even looked at them, the clothes they wore (unrecognizable brand names and faded colors) told me they were new immigrants. They must have transferred in recently, because I'd never seen them before, much less had a chance to talk to them yet.

Andromeda was a small town surrounded by fields and mountains, connected to the bigger cities by I-15. Like a little oasis. We still had things like a mall and a library, though. It was the perfect place to transition into America—or *the US*, as my mom insisted I call it, because the whole continent was America.

Maybe the girl felt me looking at her because she turned to me and held my eyes for a long time, as if she wanted to figure out my story. I held her gaze, testing my defenses, until I was too uncomfortable and looked down. And then a prickly feeling on my neck made me look over my shoulder, and to my complete surprise, there was Maverick at the door looking at me.

"Literally, Miranda," Mr. Beck said. "Don't try to copy your neighbor now."

I turned back to lay out my hatred on the puniest, most clueless teacher ever. But before I could give him a piece of my temper, Maverick said, "Mr. Beck, I'm actually here because Mrs. Santos is going to announce the cast and asked for Minnie to join us."

The cast! And Mrs. Santos had asked for me!

My hands flew to my face in surprise, but I composed myself in time. I couldn't show this much emotion to these kids or worst, the clueless teacher.

Maybe it would be better if I said I wouldn't go. Now that I thought about it, after the disaster at auditions, it was pretty obvious that I hadn't made it. There was no way I got the part of Wendy. And if I wasn't Wendy, I couldn't be anything else. I'd been so stupid, thinking that after Wendy, I could one day play Angelica or Vanessa.

Maverick smiled at me, like he expected my undying gratitude for saving me from English class. One conversation on the way to school and he thought we were best buds?

Mr. Beck looked at me like it was my fault we'd been interrupted. "Well," he stammered. "Can't the reveal wait until after the period's over?"

"Period. . . ." Ravi whispered, and the whole class snickered.

I smiled behind my I-don't-care mask.

Mr. Beck looked about to burst into flames. His face was splotchy. "Literally, Miranda. You arrive late. You leave early. You couldn't care less, now could you?"

That did it.

The chair scraped the floor when I stood up. The new girl and I made eye contact, and my mask slipped for a second, because she winked, and I couldn't help but smile. This exchange of smiles fueled my bravery, or stupidity, depending on who told the tale.

"I finished the whole quiz," I said, and handed him the piece of paper.

He smirked, but one glance on the paper stopped the mean words I was sure he wanted to say. "This looks okay, Miranda. Literally." *Cough, cough.* "Next time answer my questions promptly. The time we wasted on the quiz could have been used to better purpose. Literally."

He let that sink in, and the mood in the room turned murderous.

"Let's go, Minnie," Maverick said. He even stretched out a hand like he was saving me. I took it—not *literally* though. I'd never, ever hold hands with a boy for as long as I lived.

I grabbed my backpack and followed him, my armpits already sweaty with nerves. Leaving the classroom, I said, "Síganme los buenos," like the Chespirito show Mamá played for the girls and me on the weekends.

As I passed the classroom windows, I saw the new kids, the out-of-place siblings, smiling openly. They must have been the only ones who understood the phrase. Chespirito was common knowledge to all Spanish-speaking families in the world, or so Mamá had said.

"What does that mean?" Maverick asked.

"Really, you've never watched *El Chavo*?"

He shook his head.

"It means 'All the good ones, follow me!'"

"I love it!" Maverick exclaimed. "All the good ones. Good what, though?"

This guy was so infuriating. Did he have to ask every little stupid question that crossed his mind?

"I don't know! Good people? Not evil?"

Maverick stopped in the middle of the hallway, right next to the posters reminding students of the presidential elections next April. IT'S NEVER TOO EARLY TO PLAN! Bailey's older sister, the current student body president, announced in the picture.

Maverick and I were just outside the auditorium doors that to me seemed like the gates to either heaven and success or eternal misery.

"If you're nervous, we can go together," Maverick said.

"Are we the last ones?"

He scoffed. "They've been waiting for you forever. I think you must have gotten a big part because Mrs. Santos insisted on you being here, too."

"*Your* being here," I corrected him.

He screwed up his face in confusion. "Me? I was here...."

Seriously? He was even more clueless than the English teacher. "For the love! Let's go in already." I reached for the door, but at the last second, I turned to him and asked, "Is my hair okay?" I hadn't had time to really brush it this morning. It must have looked like a dark cloud of fluff.

I shouldn't have asked. He looked like he'd rather eat a bumblebee than answer me.

"Never mind!"

His hand clasped mine before I yanked the door open. "I was going to say that your hair looks awesome. You have something on your face, though."

He swiped something off my cheek, and I held my breath, not wanting to breathe into his face.

"There. It's some kind of glitter. It's not completely gone, but it's more toward your eye, so it looks like you have some cool makeup."

"Makeup!" I rubbed my hand against my skin, not knowing if I was making it worse or not. Never in my life, not even when I was Kota's age, had I even played with makeup. Mamá didn't wear any. Why would I bother?

"Is it really bad?"

Maverick pressed his lips together, and I had no idea if it was so he wouldn't laugh or what. But he didn't get to answer. The door flew open, almost slamming my face.

It was the Black kid I'd seen with Maverick. The one that looked like a movie star. His name was Blessings.

"Mav! We've been waiting forever!" Then he saw me and said, "There you are! Come in!"

He grabbed my arm and pretty much dragged me inside the auditorium where half the school was waiting.

When I passed the row where Bailey Cooper was surrounded by her entourage, her flowery perfume tickled my nose. She had a headband with an enormous flower perched just on top of her ear. As far as I knew, only babies were allowed decorations like that. Somehow, Bailey could pull it off. Had I ever worn anything like it? If I had, did I look as pretty as Bailey?

"Newcomers, find a seat," Mrs. Santos said over the microphone. The screech of feedback luckily switched everyone's attention away from me. I scuttled to the only empty seat on the last row.

The distraction didn't keep me out of the radar though. "Minerva, sit closer to the front," Mrs. Santos said.

I had no other choice but to follow Maverick. He was in the front row, kind of to the side of the room, so he had a perfect view of everyone while at the same time being safe from their prying eyes.

"First law of invisibility: remain in the open. It's easier to blend in," he said with his eyes fixed on Mrs. Santos.

"You don't necessarily blend in," I noted.

"Exactly." He chewed on his thumbnail, unfazed by my killer stare. "I don't. I love being unique. Like you."

How did he have the ability to say the wrong thing all the time? Or the right thing, if his aim was to make me shut up. Not even Mamá had mastered this technique.

Mrs. Santos, the microphone finally fixed, spoke again. "First of all, remember: you get what you get and you don't throw a fit."

What were we, in preschool?

The teacher continued, "Now, I'll go over the technical and set crews. Nothing would be possible without their hard work."

What she meant was that technical and set crews were the unwanted jobs. No one ever applied for them because who wanted to prepare a whole show and then work in obscurity setting up, dismounting, even cleaning up when the actors (even those without lines) received all the credit? Not me. When people noticed how well-behaved my sisters and I were, they always complimented Mamá, but it was me who did all the work.

Mamá was gone.

She was gone. What were we going to do?

The dark blanket of doom pressed down on me, suffocating me. I bit my lip as hard as I could without drawing blood. Lately, this had been my only way to prevent myself from crying.

"It's not that bad," Maverick said, and he grabbed my hand. "You're cold as ice! Are you okay? What part did you try out for?"

He knew perfectly well, but Maverick's dark eyes lasered on me until I had to look away. Because he seemed like he cared, and that was the most dangerous part of all. If there was a way to share this hurt, I would. But he was just a kid from a good family. He didn't need to have my worries thrown on his shoulders. I could carry my own burdens by myself.

"I want to be Wendy. I know all the lines."

He shrugged, but instead of saying, "Not a chance, girl!" he said, "Whatever you get, you'll be awesome." He smiled, a sunshiny kind of smile, the kind that could light up a room.

"I just don't want a technical part," I mumbled because Mrs. Santos was staring at us, apparently waiting for us to stop talking.

"Stop talking, you two!" Blessings said from behind us. He slapped Maverick's arm playfully.

"Can I start, Mr. Parker?" Mrs. Santos asked, and without waiting for a reply she started going over a list of names. When she said, "Maverick Sorensen," my mouth dropped open. Maverick would have been the perfect Peter Pan. He even had a pointy nose. Most importantly, he had the personality—the flair, Mamá would call it. But he was brown, like me. Was that why Mrs. Santos had not cast him as Peter?

Miss Santos continued firing off names, and I took the chance to lean close to Maverick and ask, "Why? Why are you on the set crew?"

"I like creating," he said, and winked at me.

I glanced behind, over my shoulder. Painted on the faces of all the kids was the widest range of emotions I'd ever seen. Some didn't look surprised at all; others were kind of bored, waiting for the announcement for the important roles. A few girls were squealing, apparently happy they were working with costumes. I envied them. I wanted a little group like that, someone to be happy with me when I got the part I wanted.

I hardly knew Maverick, but after our first conversation, he'd made an effort to be nice. Having someone in my corner cheering for me was a different kind of experience, and I kind of liked it.

"Johnny and Michael: Luke Stacey and Spencer Howell."

An explosion of cheers startled me. A seventh and an eighth grader that were obviously friends jumped in their chairs and high-fived each other.

"They're on the same soccer team," Maverick explained. "I went to elementary with them. But wait, I don't remember you from elementary. Where did you go?"

"We lived in Provo," I said, not looking at him, my eyes glued to the celebrating people.

"Ooh! Provo. How exotic!" he said, wiggling his eyebrows. "All those college students from all over the world sure make it diverse."

"It was okay," I said, trying to ignore that he'd said the E word. Maybe seeing I wasn't in the mood for jokes, he shut up.

Meanwhile, Mrs. Santos went on and on with the unimportant parts. A bunch of pirates. The fairies. The Indians. Seriously. As if Native Americans were magical creatures. Didn't Mrs. Santos realize how racist it was that there were still Indians in the play? The mermaids, at least, were mythical beings besides being stupid. They were in love with Peter, like everyone else.

And pirates? Pirates were real, even today, but people could choose to be one or not. Not the same with Native Americans. The vice-principal, Mrs. Burke, was Navajo. She was new to the school this year too. What would she think when she saw kids playing Indians like her people were magical creatures?

While these thoughts swirled in my mind, I sat still, listening with my whole body, and when I didn't hear my name, I relaxed a little.

"Now to the more demanding parts. Because we're only doing three presentations, there is one person for each of the main roles. This requires commitment and integrity. If you can't fulfill these roles with one hundred percent of your capacity, then please let me know at the end of the announcements and mention a possible alternate. This show is everyone's responsibility, and if I'm not smart enough to cast it well, then let me know."

She took a long breath and finally said, "As Hook, Canyon Smith. Wendy is Bailey Cooper. Peter is Blessings Parker, and our Tiger Lily, Minerva Miranda!"

Chapter 7

Friendly Spirits

*I*f Mrs. Santos had punched me in the mouth, I wouldn't have been more shocked.

Blessings gave a loud hoot and hugged Maverick as if he'd been selected for the Broadway *Peter Pan* and not the tiny production at Andromeda Junior High.

Of course Bailey Cooper was Wendy. She had it all. She was already perfect. Perfect face, perfect parents, perfect life. I could see her being a bright star all the way to adulthood.

My dream of living in the White House and being the first Latina president dimmed. What had I been thinking? Someone like me, being Wendy? Being the president of the United States? I couldn't believe I'd been so stupid.

Then it dawned on me. How would I tell Mamá when she came back? She'd hate for me to be Tiger

Lily. She'd been right. I should've found another route to the White House. Why had I put myself in this mess?

Mrs. Santos had cast a Black boy as Peter. She wanted to subvert stereotypes, but had she considered the message of a Black Peter Pan renouncing his eternal, happy childhood for a white girl?

But then, why had she cast *me* as Tiger Lily? Because I was dark-skinned?

The more people congratulated me for being Tiger Lily (*You're perfect! You look just like her!*), the angrier I became.

A storm brewed inside me. The kind that leaves only destruction behind.

No,

no,

no.

I was not going to be the subservient, silent princess. She was the Chief of the Indians, but in the play, she didn't do anything else but love Peter!

Her name was even more ridiculous than mine.

Mrs. Santos was putting her papers away in a Super Mario bag. She had a smile of satisfaction, like she was a fairy godmother, pleased with the gifts she'd endowed upon her lowly students.

Not me, though. I wouldn't play her game.

"Mrs. Santos," I said, intercepting her escape.

"Congratulations," she said, extending a hand for me to shake.

I took it because I was angry, not stupefied. A teacher was a teacher, no matter how wrong, how clueless, how cruel.

"I didn't audition for Tiger Lily." I made an effort to control my voice, but I was having a hard time breathing evenly.

"But you're perfect for her," Miss Santos said, handing me the script.

I glanced down at it. Tiger Lily's line—one line—was highlighted. She said only "How" and made some motions with her hands, and then she danced to that stupid song.

Fifty dollars for this. Oh, plus the fee for costume rental. It wasn't included in the audition fee.

"Aren't you excited?" Mrs. Santos asked.

Maverick stood behind her, kind of to the side. I didn't want an audience, but it was now or never.

"I don't want to offend you," I said. "But I won't play Tiger Lily."

"Why not?" Bailey Cooper asked as she came bounding in our direction. Mrs. Santos beamed at her, but Bailey's eyes were trained on me. "Minerva, you'll be perfect. And your mom can surely do wonders with your hair if you let her," she said, brushing a hand over my puffy hair. "Her mom is wonderful doing hair, Mrs. Santos," Bailey added, turning toward the teacher.

Good thing, because every time Bailey even mentioned my mom, I wanted to go into Ursula-from-*The-Little-Mermaid* mode and destroy the world. Bailey had the nerve to talk about my mom as if she knew her. Did she know where my mom was? Should I have asked her?

Oh, Mamá, come back home! I need you!

A ringing silence alerted me that Mrs. Santos and Bailey were staring at me.

"There's no need to cry," said Mrs. Santos, patting my arm. My sorrow would take way more than patting to go away. "It's just a play, sweetheart. You don't always get the part that you want, as we don't in real life. We all need to compromise. I didn't know you felt so strongly against sweet Tiger Lily. I do feel you'd be perfect, but if you disagree, I'll let you drop out of the play if you find a replacement. That's the rule."

Rules? What did she know about rules?

There were real rules, like children shouldn't have to play mom and dad when their parents disappear, or you shouldn't have to constantly prove you're worth playing the lead role even when you're darker-skinned.

But Mrs. Santos knew nothing.

First of all, I wasn't about to cry.

Second of all, I didn't feel strongly against Tiger Lily.

I. Did. Not. Care. About. Stupid. Tiger. Lily.

I wanted to be Wendy. That was it.

I'd already been cheated in real life, and now the play? I wanted to have a shot at the student body presidency elections, for goodness sake!

And third, and most important of all, I wanted Bailey Cooper to stop talking about my mom as if she had any claim to her. Even if my mom had worked for her, she hadn't belonged to Bailey. She was mine. *My mom.* Even if she was gone.

"I feel strongly that there should be no Tiger Lily," I said, trying not to shake. "She doesn't even say anything other than 'How.' And the Indians? They act nothing like real Native people."

The silence in the room made my ears ring. Bailey Cooper avoided my eyes like I'd become a monster too horrible to look at. Mrs. Santos placed a hand over her heart and whispered, "I hadn't thought of it that way."

All around us, the sound of whispers escalated. "How can she say that?" "Everything has to be politically correct." "Get over it!" "But it's a classic. . . ."

I couldn't tell who said what.

"What do you propose?" Mrs. Santos asked. She sounded like she meant it, like she was really interested in what I had to say. She was a good woman, but why was it me who had to come up with a solution? She was the teacher.

As I thought of a solution, I remembered something Mamá had said weeks ago when we'd argued about the play. Something about a theater group destroying the stereotypes in Peter Pan, but I didn't remember the details. I'd only been fixated on Wendy. I hadn't cared about Tiger Lily.

Now I didn't even care about the play.

My family had left the church because of a play, but I couldn't leave the school, could I? No. No middle school dropout had become the president of the United States.

"I'll find something," I said. It sounded like a promise.

Mrs. Santos nodded slowly, turned on her heels, and left, followed by her perfect students, Bailey Cooper among them.

What had I gotten myself into?

I turned around and left the auditorium. Maverick followed me.

When I reached the cafeteria, though, I kept walking. Not even the decadent smell of pizza could stop me. I walked past the English classroom. I crossed the hallway, went down the stairs into a part of the school I'd never been to, and crossed to a door, walking all the way to the sunshine outside.

The crisp mountain air cleared my thoughts a little. What had I done? Maverick stood next to me, as if I needed another shadow.

"Can you believe how ridiculous the stupid play is?" I asked. My voice shook. "And my line? *How.* That's all Tiger Lily says. Indians don't talk like that. It's so wrong!"

Maverick, his face flushed, his longish hair falling over his eyes, shrugged one shoulder. "Mrs. Santos was interested in what you said. I saw it on her face. Could you tell she actually heard what you had to say? If you find a solution, this could be historic."

"It was all rigged. The tryouts, you know?"

That was the only explanation for the stupid casting choices. "Why even bother with tryouts if she already knew who should play what?"

"Blessings got Peter Pan. No one saw that curve ball coming," Maverick said.

I had no idea what a curve ball was, but even then, yeah. I didn't see that coming. Blessings as Peter?

"Maybe she had, like, a diversity quota to fill and by picking Blessings she thought she was doing her part to be fair to humanity. But guess what? I won't have it. I won't be part of her quota!"

Maverick picked a blade of grass and chewed it. Didn't he know they sprayed the fields with insecticide and fertilizer?

Before I could enlighten him, he said, "Last year a white girl played Tiger Lily. She reminded me a little of you, the way she acted. But anyway, her parents almost ate Mrs. Santos alive. So, I can understand why this year she chose you because you were the only one who fit the physical description. I think her choosing Blessings as Peter is going to be a kick in the you-know-what for the PTA, but what are they going to say if they don't want to come across as racist? The bravest thing she could have done was pick up a girl to play Peter, but I'm afraid our school isn't ready for that yet. Even though girls have always played Peter in the big shows."

As he talked, the nebula of an idea started forming in my mind. It was almost there. I could feel it, but just as I tried to grasp it, it vanished. I needed silence and time to think. "Is our school ready for a Peter Pan without Indians?" I wondered. "That's what I want to know."

"No Indians? But they're part of the tradition. Peter Pan's a classic," he said, sounding just like all those people complaining.

"No representation is better than harmful representation, my mom always says."

Maverick didn't argue. Maybe the words of a mom had more power than *tradition*. "I'm sorry," he said. "I know nothing. I'm a coconut: brown on the outside, white on the inside. That's what Blessings says sometimes, anyway."

My anger cooled to a simmering broth. Oh, Maverick. A coconut? I would have laughed, but he sounded so, so sad.

"Blessings is a cool name," I said, because I hated the pressure in my chest when the silence rang around me again. "How loved would a person feel if they were called Blessings?"

"His parents are from Ghana, and those names are common there," Maverick said in a soft voice. "His older brother died in a four-wheeling accident right before Blessings was born."

A blessed baby after losing another. Such sorrow. I imagined losing either of my sisters. No name would ever make up for their loss.

Maverick's comment reminded me I wasn't the only one who went through hard things. I'd only been thinking of my situation, without looking around, which wasn't what a good president-of-the-country-in-training should do.

I needed a break. I needed to recoup, calm down, and analyze the situation before I let myself be governed by emotion. The grass on the soccer fields was still damp and moisture seeped through the sole of my shoes.

I couldn't go back to class and face everyone. Feeling rebellious, I left the school. Maverick followed me.

How long did he plan on walking with me?

"What does your name mean?" I asked to redirect the conversation.

Maverick ruffled my hair. "Look it up, goddess. You must feel pretty special knowing your mom named you after the goddess of wisdom."

First of all, I didn't know if I should pulverize him on the spot for daring to touch my hair or for making a stupid comment about my name.

But poor, clueless Maverick. He had no idea. My story and the story of my name weren't as inspiring as Blessings's. I laughed.

According to my mom, my dad had named me because he had a girlfriend before Mamá who was named Minerva. Mamá hadn't known until a friend of his broke the news after Papá left us, but the damage was already done. I'd already been Minerva for six years by then.

My name reminded Mamá she hadn't been Papá's first pick. That made me feel *awesome*.

I couldn't tell Maverick all this, and he just smiled, maybe wondering what I was thinking about. His braces had green bands.

Lucky. I'd have to do something about my overbite before I ran for president of the country, that's for sure.

"My name means *free spirit*," Maverick said, circling with his arms open wide, as if he were hugging the world. I watched him until he stopped, and then he wobbled to my side. I groaned, but secretly, I wished I had the guts to be silly in public. Like him.

"Who named you that?"

His smile flickered a little, and he lowered his eyes. "My birth mom. Her one condition was that my parents would keep the names she'd chosen: Maverick Leonel. Maverick after a character from a movie she liked, and Leonel after her favorite brother."

At *birth mother*, I went cold, like someone had dumped a bucket of ice water on me.

Maverick didn't notice I'd frozen, and continued, "I know nothing else about her besides that she insisted on my name, and the fact that she was Latina. But I don't know anything about what kind of Latina, or even what country she came from— *if* she was even from another country. My parents are awesome, but . . . sometimes I wonder if I'm missing a side of me, you know? I can't even speak Spanish."

He kicked a ball that had been forgotten on the field. The ball landed on the white line, waiting there like it didn't want to break the rules, teetering on the verge of obedience and truancy.

Was that why Maverick hung out with me? Because I was a Latina?

Maverick and I looked at each other. He gave me a crooked smile, but his eyes were so deep and sad.

Like Kota's. He and I crossed the white boundary of the soccer field at the same time.

"Where are we going?" he asked, changing the subject.

Alarms went off in my mind. "We?"

He shrugged. "Yep. Where are we heading?"

"I'm getting my little sister from day care," I said. I hadn't left the school with the intention of rescuing Avi from the evil Mirta, but now this seemed like the only thing to do.

"Cool," he said, "I have tons of older sisters but not little ones."

"They're a pain." This was the worst lie I had ever told. Horrible, untrue words, but there was no way to take them back.

Apparently, I was such a bad liar, Maverick waved off the lie like a fly. "No, your sisters are too cute to be a pain. They look like you."

We were almost at the day care place, and I didn't have time to analyze his ridiculous words. This boy! Why did he say the things he said? I didn't know how to talk to him.

Right then, my stomach rumbled with hunger, reminding me that today I hadn't especially demonstrated the best judgment. I should've taken advantage of the school lunch, at least to bring something for Avi. I had fifty dollars in my backpack, though.

Fifty that could have been one hundred if I hadn't wasted half on the play fee.

If I explained the situation to her when I was calmer, would Mrs. Santos give me back the fee money? She had to.

But I'd worry about that after I dealt with Mirta. The evil witch.

"Wait here," I said.

Maverick stood in the middle of the sidewalk like there was nowhere else in the world he'd rather be. A police car cruised by and Maverick saluted insolently. The officer waved coolly.

The door opened before I knocked. Mirta stood there, crossing her arms and *tsk*ing at me. I checked my watch. Mickey Mouse's arms were pointing exactly at noon. I was three hours early.

"She's being a stinker today," Mirta said. "She won't stop crying. She's been in the time-out chair for a long time, but she doesn't get the message."

The time-out chair? Toddlers can't learn anything from a time out! They're too little. I clamped my teeth tightly so the bad words wouldn't escape.

But I hoped Mirta could see how I imagined her like a cockroach, stomped to smithereens. Just the same size as her soul.

Before I could give her a piece of my mind, Avi ran and hugged my leg. I bent down to pick her up. Her hair reeked of cigarette smoke. Swear words in both English and Spanish crowded in my mouth.

Without a word or a second look at the evil witch, I turned around, hating the fact that tomorrow, I'd have to swallow my pride and come back. Leave my sweet Avi, again.

But, no. I couldn't do it. I wouldn't do it.

"Let's go, baby," I whispered in her ear. I must have tickled her because she shrugged and smiled the tiniest smile I'd ever seen, even for her tiny face.

From behind me, Mirta called, "Tell your mom your sister needs more diapers. We're out!"

I didn't deign to turn around and acknowledge the fact that she'd talked to me. If anything, I wanted to do a rude gesture with my fingers. But what would we do then? What would Mamá say if Mirta went to her with the gossip that I had cut school and then come to her house to disrespect her? Better to ignore her, even though my anger level was volcano-eruption high.

"Everything okay?" Maverick asked.

I so wish I could talk to him like he'd talked about his birth mother before, but I didn't really know him. I couldn't trust him yet.

"It's okay," I just said.

"Hi, beautiful!" he said to my baby sister in a tone of voice that shouldn't be allowed. Did boys take lessons for this?

Avi's face lit up at the sound of his voice. She squinted her eyes and smiled, showing teeth and all. The little stinker was a flirt.

Maverick, the king of flirts, batted his eyes at her. "She likes me," he said. "Can I hold her?"

By the time I was halfway through saying, "Nah, she never goes with strangers," she'd practically jumped off my arms and nestled in his.

Maverick and I laughed. "Let's go to the gas station," I said. "We need milk and bread."

Chapter 8

The Case Against the Mouse

I WAS USUALLY REALLY good at hiding the fact that I was an adult hiding in the body of an underdeveloped, badly dressed twelve-year-old. Something about Maverick made me wish I could just act like a kid, just for a little while. So at the gas station, I bought milk, peanut butter, bread, and a small bag of gummy bears. For the girls, I told myself. They deserved a little sweetness.

When I paid, though, I was still surprised at the total price and regretted the decision to buy candy. It was too late now. The gas station wasn't the cheapest place, but it was the only one I could walk to.

"Where to now?" Maverick asked, letting Avi play with his hair while I fought with the milk jug that didn't want to stay inside my backpack.

"It's Kota's early-out day. Let's go get her," I said, ignoring my grumbling stomach.

Technically she could walk home by herself, but what if something happened to her just because I wanted to go home and eat something?

"Let's wait here," I said, stopping on the corner right next to the kindergarten playground so Avi could have a go or two on the slide.

She ran ahead, like a puppy with two tails. "A fairy!" she exclaimed.

"What fairy, baby?" I glanced quickly at Maverick, worried that he'd think Avi was a little cuckoo.

She pointed at something. There was only a beam of sunshine playing tricks on the transparent plastic that connected two sections of the slide.

"Where?" I squinted, but whatever she was pointing at was invisible to me.

"There, Minnie. Fairy!"

She squealed in delight and ran with her little arms in the air, an expression of complete joy I didn't want to ruin just because *I* didn't see the fairy.

Inside the plastic tunnel, Avi mumbled in a language all of her own.

"What's she saying?" Maverick asked.

I shrugged. "Avalonish, I guess. It's not Spanish, in case you're wondering."

"What I was wondering is more along the lines of who she's talking to," Maverick said. He looked at Avi with longing. "When do you think we grow out of that? I used to be just like her. I don't know when I changed."

I'd never been like that. I'd always had someone to take care of. When it wasn't the girls, it had been Mamá.

Like now. Where was my mom? "I guess we grow up when we need to take care of ourselves. I don't know."

Maverick shook his head as if saying *not that*.

"Do you cut class a lot to take care of your sisters? What about your parents?"

"You don't understand," I said, standing with my arms crossed like a shield between me and this boy who'd never known responsibility in his life. "My mom's a single mom and she works full time. I have to help out. Don't you?"

He laughed. "Are you kidding me? I'm the youngest of seven. The only boy. The dream son my parents prayed to God for for years until He sent me. I rule the world. At least the world in my house."

I closed my eyes for a second trying to imagine

what that kind of life must have been like. But I couldn't even catch a glimpse of an alternate-world Minerva, one that didn't have to worry about where her next meal was coming from.

"The dream child, huh?" That's all I could say.

"I'm adopted—I told you before. My parents chose me, and my birth mother chose them."

Two mothers who loved him. And then all of those sisters. Talk about luck.

"You're lucky. You have a wonderful life."

He looked up at me and his eyes were shiny. "I do. I also lost a lot, you know? I know nothing about my culture. I can't speak Spanish. My parents try, but . . . it's just too hard."

"But they try," I said, feeling like I had to defend his parents, because at the end of the day, they were there for him. Where was *my* mom?

"Won't your mom wonder where you are right now?" I asked, remembering that he'd cut school to be with me. Would I get into trouble because he'd followed me?

"Nope!"

"Don't you have places to be? What about sports?"

"Nope and nope. Not on Tuesdays."

This wasn't working. But before I got rid of him,

I had to ask. "Why didn't they cast a Tinker Bell in the play?" Before Tiger Lily, I'd happily be Tinker Bell a million times over.

He swiped his hair to the side and went all business mode, apparently happy I'd changed the subject. "That's what's so cool about being in the tech crew. *We* are Tinker Bell." He looked at me, waiting for me to get it. But I didn't get it. Did he want to dress up in pointy slippers and a skimpy green dress?

"What? All the kids are Tinker Bell?"

He laughed, slapping his leg as if I had told the joke of the century. "No! Tinker Bell is too magical to be played by a person. She's light and music. We create her—the tech crew, I mean."

"But why?" I didn't see Avi from where I stood, but she was still blabbering and giggling.

Maverick was oblivious to my sister's imaginary talk with a fairy. Now that he was talking about the play, he was all worked up. "Magical things happen when people use their imaginations. We don't even practice Tinker Bell's parts during rehearsals, but every time, things come out beautifully. At least they did last year, when I was in seventh."

Avi ran to Maverick right then and hugged his legs.

I was a little embarrassed and I don't know why. She was three years old, after all.

"Mavvy nice. Fairy nice."

"Okay, say goodbye to my friend, Avi," I said before she invited Maverick to come over to our house.

But he tickled Avi until she belly-laughed.

"I can hang out," he said.

"Well," I said, "*my mom* doesn't let me hang out on school nights. See you tomorrow."

He stood up, holding Avi with his left arm, and placed his free hand over his heart, taking a step back. "Ouch," he gasped, "are you trying to shake *me* off? This hasn't happened to me since . . . since . . . since I don't know when."

"How tragic. Sorry," I mumbled, taking Avi from his arms. "See you tomorrow."

Kota was running our way. Her eyes went huge when she saw Maverick by my side.

Maverick saw her too, and winked at her. "Cute little sisters. This one looks just like you." He patted my shoulder like I was a guy, one of his friends. "Before you kick me out again, I'll save my feelings. See you tomorrow, Tiger Lily."

And he left. Left me speechless on the sidewalk.

☆ 111 ☆

"Was that a guy?" Kota asked, as if she had never seen a boy in her life. For us, boys were strange creatures, more mythical than unicorns.

Like she was telling me off for being rude, Avi whispered, "Minniiiie . . ."

"I didn't kick him out, Avi," I said, my cheeks burning. "We can't let people in. Not yet."

My sisters were lost in their thoughts. It wasn't fair that a six-year-old and a toddler had to worry so much. That was my job. I could take the worries. I was strong enough.

But my determination to make things right for my sisters was crowded with question marks, all following images of our mother, the play, our next meal, rent that was due in two weeks.

And then Kota exclaimed, "It's out! My tooth just fell out!" She put her hand in her mouth and took out the freshly fallen tooth. She held it up for the sun to kiss.

"Oh," I said, and in a move I didn't completely understand, I held up my hand, my palm facing up. A tendril of blood still connected the tooth to Kota's mouth.

Kota's face crumpled as she struggled not to cry, and she handed me the bloody tooth.

Around us the world moved like nothing had happened. Kids greeted their mothers. Birds flew and sang. The mountain breeze tangled my already messy hair. I stood there with a tooth in my hand and two little sisters waiting for me to be their mom.

Usually the sight of blood made me sick. This time, the nausea I was expecting never came. I kissed the top of Kota's head. Her hair smelled of sunshine. She sobbed against my arm, angling her body so the other kids on the sidewalk wouldn't see her cry.

"It's okay," I shushed her. "It's okay, Dakota."

She sniffled. "A part of me wanted it to fall out when Mamá came back," she said, her voice choky, "but in a way, I'm so happy it fell out now!"

"Why?"

She covered her face, but I still heard her words. "I don't want the Mouse to come."

I almost laughed, but I bit my lip instead.

"The Mouse only comes in Argentina."

"In Spain, too," she exclaimed, the fury in her still hot in spite of the tears. "It was in that book. . . . He goes to Puerto Rico, too. Besides, you said . . ."

I had said she'd get the Mouse. I had been mean. She needed me now. "We moved houses, remember? The Tooth Fairy has jurisdiction here, you see?" I said, in a voice that didn't sound like me really. It was too soft.

Kota—gentle, forgiving Kota—played along. She nodded, brushing her tears from her cheeks, like she'd known all along and only needed my reassurance. "What about the Peques? If they're fairies from Argentina, how come they gave us cupcakes here in America?"

"The Peques actually came from Europe and Asia and all over the world. Remember Mamá said they traveled in people's suitcases when they crossed the ocean?"

Kota grabbed my elbow, and we started walking again. "They came in Mamá's suitcases when she came to the States?"

I took a long breath. Someone was barbecuing, and the smell made my mouth water. "They came in Papá's, I think. Mamá grew up here."

"Not here," Kota corrected. "She grew up in Miami."

"I meant this country. The Peques followed Papá."

"Is that why they're taking care of us now that he and Mami are gone?"

We walked on the sidewalk at three-year-old-mesmerized-by-fall-leaves speed, which is no speed at all. I picked up Avi. We still needed to stop by the community garden if we wanted to eat tonight. Besides, I didn't know how to answer Kota's questions. Between her and Maverick and the quiz in English class, my mind was about to explode.

"We're stopping by the garden first," I said to distract her from questions.

"Okay," they both replied.

"Jinx!" I exclaimed, and they laughed.

My stomach rumbled again. Even if their tiny stomachs were quiet, they had to be hungry too. I had to do something. How do you explain to a hungry three-year-old that there's no food in the house?

The community garden gate was locked with a chain, and I tried to open it, but it didn't budge.

"¿Volvemos después?" Kota asked.

When I looked up, I saw why she wanted to keep our plan of coming back later a secret. The lady in charge of the garden watched us like we were criminals. We'd come to pick up produce with Mamá in the past, and the lady hadn't been nice. Once, she'd been talking to another woman, and in a voice loud enough for me to hear, she said that it was unfair that *people who never contributed got to reap the fruits of her labor*. Her actual words.

I didn't understand. Wasn't a community garden supposed to be for the community?

Avi waved at her, but instead of smiling or at least opening the gate, the woman turned her back to us. Who does that? I wished for super powers so all of her plump and ripe vegetables would go to waste before she could taste them, for caterpillars and crickets to swarm down on her bounty and eat it all. She looked healthy enough; she had plenty to eat. Why wouldn't she share?

"Yes, let's come back later," I said, knowing that there was no way we'd come back later, or ever.

My sisters knew it too, by the looks on their faces.

With a fist in the air, Kota called out against the injustice. "You meanie! You're the meanest!"

"It's okay, Kota," I said. "We want to behave so the Tooth Fairy can visit you tonight."

That's all I needed to say. In a blink, her angry expression switched to an angelical one.

We finally made it home without questions about pesky Peques or mean people who didn't really care about anyone but themselves. "I hungry, Minnie," Avi said, tugging at my shirt.

I made peanut butter toast and gave her a handful of gummy bears. She clapped and hopped in place.

After she ate, she tugged at my shirt again. "Pee, pee, Sissy." Kota, who was polishing her tooth on the kitchen countertop, sent me a pleading look.

"Oh, well," I said, and took Avi's hand and headed to the bathroom.

"Good luck, Minerva! Better you than me."

"Kota, watch it, or the fairy won't bring you anything!" I couldn't think of a worse threat. I knew how it hurt when the Tooth Fairy didn't show up.

"You nice like fairy, Minnie. She my friend, too, Minnie," Avi said.

I imagined she must have been thinking about my conversation with Kota. She was smarter than I gave her credit for. Still, when Mamá came back, I'd have a talk with her about the girls' obsessions with fairies. This wasn't healthy.

🔆·🔆·🔆

After the bathroom break, which was horrible as always, I sat my sister down with a pile of books.

"I have to do homework now, Avi, okay? And then I have to get our clothes ready for school tomorrow."

Avi's face went from utter bliss to total panic when

I mentioned the word school. "No Mirta, Minnie. She mean. No Mirta, pleath. . . ."

That evil witch! Avi couldn't go back to that horrible woman, but I couldn't miss school. Maybe if Kota and I switched days? If we took turns going to school? But no, after a couple of absences the school would call, both hers and mine. Besides, Kota was too young to stay home alone with Avi.

What to do with the baby? Why couldn't she come to school with me? She was so well-behaved; she wouldn't bother anyone at all.

"Let me think about it, okay? I still need to wash your underwear and see what Kota and I are going to eat for dinner."

"I'm going to get a flower for my fairy," Kota said, just when I was about to ask her for ideas.

Alarms went off in my head. "Where?"

She pointed out the window. I couldn't see a thing from here.

"Just outside. I need my alone time," she said. "I don't wanna fight, Minerva Soledad. Be nice. I just lost a tooth. I'm emotional, okay?"

If she had another tantrum, I wouldn't have the patience to deal with it. The day was still nice outside. A change of air would do her good.

"Okay, you can go get a flower, but come back inside straight away in case someone sees you by yourself and wonders where Mamá is."

Kota's eyes went wide. "Or Mamá could come back, and then she'll see I've been disobedient and walk out on us again. You're right. I'll be out and in."

She went out before I could correct her. I don't know how, but I had a suspicion Mamá wouldn't come back today, either. And even if she came back, I'm sure telling Kota off for being outside wasn't even right after being gone for so long. And no, she hadn't walked out on us. I knew that just as certainly as I knew the sun would shine tomorrow.

I sat to do my homework because I knew that after today's English quiz, Mr. Beck would want to catch me unprepared again. I wouldn't give him the satisfaction. Avi was busy playing with her blocks while I worked.

The door creaked behind me. A cold presence stood there, and when I heard the heavy footsteps on the carpet, my heart went loud like conga drums.

I turned around, ready to forgive, ready to pretend these two days hadn't happened. "Mamá!" I exclaimed.

But when my eyes adjusted to the semi-darkness

of the room, I saw it was just Kota standing in the doorway, her arms full of vegetables and fruits. She looked like a harvest fairy.

"Oh, it's you," I said, hating the fact that she'd seen me get excited. She'd probably also seen the look of disappointment I wasn't quick enough to push back into my soul.

Avi left her blocks and hugged me. The darker my thoughts, the quieter my sister had become.

How I wished Mamá would walk into the apartment and see how we needed her. How I wanted to tell her about the stupid play and ask her about the dress that had been Bailey's.

"Where did you get that?" I asked my sister, because I couldn't tell Kota what I was really thinking about.

"Mr. Chang gave it to me." Kota placed the fruit in the largest bowl we owned. She arranged the apples, the carrots with the tops attached, the bright orange squash carefully, like they were jewels. They were beautiful. No produce at the store looked anything like this.

I closed my books, took an apple, and smelled it. The sweet tartness of it made my tongue tingle. "Why would he give this to you?"

She blushed again. This girl couldn't lie. "He saw me picking apples from the ground."

"Kota!" I protested, putting the apple away fast as if it could burn. "You shouldn't have done that!"

"They were on the ground." She stomped her foot for emphasis. "No one would've missed them. Besides, he said it was totally fine for us to take whatever we wanted."

"Ay, Kota!" I sighed, plopping down on the couch. The weight on my shoulders was too heavy for my puny legs. "We can't let anyone know that Mamá isn't here. They'll call Social Services. What if they take you away?"

"And you?"

"They'd never catch me. I'd run away and then come rescue you. You poopy-head, what do you think?" I hid my face behind my hands so she couldn't see how upset I was in spite of my words. Because honestly, what could I really do if someone took us away?

Kota took my hands and knelt in front of me so I could see her face, or she could see mine. "Minerva, maybe we need someone to look for her. What if she's in danger? What if she never comes back?"

The fact that I'd been thinking about this all day

didn't make me feel any better. "What if Mr. Chang's a bad man? What if he hurts you?"

"He's okay," she said waving her hand in the air. "He let me alone in the garden to get whatever I wanted. He said he never had such beautiful produce until we moved in. That we brought him the good harvest spirits. That when the cold weather starts everything will go to waste. That there's no way he could eat it all. And now that I think about it, how lonely he must be. Maybe he wants to adopt us. Like your friend Maverick's adopted."

I'd never given our neighbor a thought. Harvest spirits? He and Mamá would get along if she ever came back. I didn't know anything about our landlord, and with what I'd heard, I preferred that he didn't know anything about us either.

"Let's tell him," Kota said. "About Mamá."

Part of me wanted to say yes. To hand over my burden to an adult. To let someone else fix this problem. But I couldn't fail Mamá. Our problems were *our* problems.

"Give me until Friday. I promise that if she isn't back by Friday, then we'll tell someone. And Kota? No one's ever going to adopt us, okay? We already have a mom."

We shook hands to seal the deal. Avi wanted to shake too, but first she spat on her palm before shaking with Kota and me. Where had she learned that from?

"Deal!" she exclaimed in her bell-like voice.

After our deal making, we ate apples and cheese. I poured cheerios in a bowl for the three of us to share. For dessert, we ate carrots. They were so sweet and tasted nothing like the grocery store kind.

Finally, Avi went to asleep. Kota lingered in the kitchen like she wanted to ask something but she didn't dare.

"Go to bed, Kota. And don't forget to leave your tooth underneath your pillow."

"Do you think—?"

"Of course she'll come. Leave her a note, but remember she might not answer with words."

"I know," she said. "I left her some milk, too." She kissed me on the cheek, and I gave her a little hug.

We always kissed Mamá at night. Now that our mother was missing, kissing duty was mine.

I waited until the girls were asleep to go rummage in Mamá's chifforobe for some clues. Maybe I'd missed something before. The faint scent of her sweet peach perfume, the one that she only wore to the doctor or a parent/teacher conference, still lingered.

I hugged her coat, her shirts. I touched the pages of her journal. She wouldn't want me to read it, but maybe in there I'd find something. Maybe she'd written, *I'm sick and tired of these girls. I'm leaving them for good.* But even as I thought it, I knew she'd never write that down. There was a power in written words. Once out in the open, they were real.

I opened a wooden box. Her wedding ring sat there in the middle, hanging from the ballerina that didn't dance anymore. Three envelopes with little clippings of hair were tucked at the bottom. They all looked the same, all the little pieces of curl. If it weren't for Mamá's writing—Minerva, Dakota, Avalon—I couldn't tell which was whose. It seemed like a lie that Kota's and mine had looked like our angel sister's. Avi's was so blonde it looked like yellow cotton candy.

I thought about the Ziploc bags full of teeth I'd found the other day, and the pang in my chest returned. I'd known for a while about the Tooth Fairy, but the discovering of the baggie brought all of my childhood to dust, and not the fairy kind. Now I knew for sure.

"It's okay," I said aloud, although there was no one to hear me. "I'm a big girl."

Quietly, I put everything away. I closed the box and hid it under a pile of blankets so my sisters wouldn't find it.

I opened Mamá's address book at a random spot. *Fátima Grant, Mamá* in bright red pulsed from the page. A phone number with too many digits to be a Utah number and an address in Rosario, Argentina, told me what I needed to know. This Fátima Grant, my grandma, was too far from us to be of any help.

Still I copied down the information on a piece of paper. Maybe she knew where my father was. Maybe she'd tell him we needed him, and he'd rescue us from this loneliness. I couldn't call her from our house, but maybe tomorrow I could go to the computer lab and look her up.

I was tucking the paper carefully in my binder when I remembered about Kota's tooth.

If Kota woke up the next day and the tooth was still there, it would be a catastrophe. I couldn't fail her!

I checked the windowsill to dump the milk and pretend the fairy had drank all of it, but the milk was already gone. Maybe Kota had forgotten after all her preparations? But no. A slimy film of recently poured milk covered the bottom of the bowl. It was like it had evaporated. Or like someone had drunk from it.

A sparkling of glitter trailed next to the window, all the way to the front door. The same glitter color as the one on Mamá's wallet.

I checked behind my sister's pillow, which wasn't hard at all, since she was sleeping across the bed. The tooth wasn't there. I searched frantically but instead of a tooth, I found a golden coin that sparkled, gleaming with magic and impossibility.

Or was it possibility?

Chapter 9

The Fairies' Favorite

"*I*SN'T THIS THE bestest thing you ever saw?" Kota said for like the millionth time. She petted that coin like it was her precious. "You never got anything like this, right?"

She hadn't aimed for it, but the arrow found my heart anyway. "No, Kota," I said. "The Mouse came for me once when Papá still lived here and left me a dollar. Maybe the Tooth Fairy got offended, because when she took my teeth, she only left me quarters."

Avi came up to me, patted my hand, and said, "Fairy nice, Minnie. She so nice!" She sucked on a lollipop. I had no idea where she'd gotten it.

Kota must have guessed the question in my eyes because she said, "It was under her pillow. Maybe the Tooth Fairy brought it to her."

Maybe it was true. But if it was, why hadn't the blasted fairy left me anything, then? Wasn't *I* still a kid? Most likely the lollipop had been wedged between the bed and the wall and Avi found it by coincidence. Again, I wouldn't say it aloud, but there were no such things as fairies or magic or miracles. Not for me anyway.

"Why aren't you ready for school?" Kota asked as she put her backpack on.

I looked at myself in the mirror. "What do you mean? I'm wearing the same stuff I wear every day."

It was true. Faded jeans and T-shirt with a hoodie on top. I hated to admit that I wore it because I didn't have a bra and I had grown, and not because I was cold. I had wanted to tell Mamá that I needed one, and now there was no one to tell. How did one go around buying that kind of thing? The gas station didn't sell training bras, that's for sure.

"I'm not going to school," I continued. "Well, I am, but Avi isn't going to Mirta's," I said. I'd thought about this plan all night, after finding the coin the fairy had left for my sister.

"Why? How?" Kota asked.

Avi looked at me in a way that made skipping school for the rest of eternity so worth it. There was no room for doubts in my heart. In the back of my mind, a voice kept repeating that I couldn't just stop attending school.

I took Avi's hand and said, "We'll walk you to school, and then Avi will go to school with me so my first period teacher can see me. Then I'll say that I'm sick. That should give me until Friday to stay home. I can sneak through a hallway door to walk out with her." The door Maverick and I had gone out through yesterday. No one had noticed us gone. I could use it again today.

"Is she coming with you? The teacher will notice her! Trust me, some teachers really do pay attention," Kota said, her eyes full of horror and a little bit of excitement. "Wait! Can I come with you guys?" When she spoke now, bits of spit flew because her smile had a window, now the tooth was gone. It was kind of cute, but gross at the same time.

"You can't come because one little girl is easier to hide than two. And the school will call if you miss more school."

Kota was way smart. She knew when she could insist and when to give in. "Okay," she conceded. "If Mamá comes back Friday, you'll go to school Monday, right?"

"Right," I said, sounding way surer than I really felt.

We headed out the door and made our trek in a heavy kind of silence. Before we reached the crossing guard, I noticed how Kota kept her hand in her pocket the whole time.

"Kota," I said. "You brought your coin! You can't tell anyone about—"

"I know!" she exclaimed. "I won't tell about Mamá."

I stared her down, and she lowered her eyes.

Yep. I still had it in me. "I wasn't going to say that. I was going to say, don't tell anyone about the coin from the Tooth Fairy," I protested.

Her face went all somber and stormy. "Peyton—"

"Your friend?"

She *tsk*ed at me. "Don't interrupt! Peyton's mom caught the Tooth Fairy on camera, and get this." She lifted a finger and her eyebrow so that I'd really get it, whatever she was about to say. "She printed out a shot of the fairy kissing Peyton. Peyton even had a tiny kiss on her cheek!"

Lies. All lies. The lengths some parents went to astounded me.

Kota was so smart, though. Couldn't she see her

friend's mom was duping them all? Us all? Silly woman. She was setting everyone up for disaster. How was one supposed to compete with a true-fake picture of the fairy caught red-handed, or red-lipped, or whatever?

With a magical golden coin, of course.

I couldn't blame Kota for wanting to bring her treasure to school. "What if you lose it?" I asked. "Remember when you lost your brand new My Little Pony—"

"Melody," Kota said.

"Yes, Melody. You brought her to the store and then you left her in the cart by accident."

That's all it took for her plan to crumble. Worst case scenario visualization was my specialty.

"Okay, you party-pooper, you!" she exclaimed. "*You* keep it safe for me."

This alternative didn't make me happy either. Now the weight of it was on me, adding to all the other things I had.

"You should have left it back home," I said. "What if *I* lose it?"

"You won't, Minnie. I trust you! Besides, if I take it, I'll be tempted to show it off. Do this for me. Please, Minnie?"

"You get me into all kinds of trouble!" I snapped at her but took the coin from her hand and placed it in my pocket.

She stayed quiet the rest of the way. Instead of a kiss, she waved her hand in my general direction and ran to catch up with a friend. But before she walked into the school, she looked over her shoulder and waved properly.

How I wished I really knew the way to Neverland after all, so I could take my sisters on a real adventure!

"No Mirta, Minnie?" Avi asked clutching my hand as tightly as she could.

If I had any doubts as to what I should do, they vanished as soon as I saw my sister's panicked eyes and heard her quivering voice.

"No poopy-head Mirta," I promised as I opened the secret door behind the garbage dumps.

Minnie laughed. It wasn't a first baby laugh, so no new fairies were born of it, but it made me feel like I had bubbles in my blood and that I walked a little lighter, although I carried my three-year-old sister.

We walked in through the hallway door, and I looked around for a place to hide my sister. And there, under the stairs, was a small unlocked room. It was dark and musty-smelling, but there was nowhere else to hide my sister for an hour or so. A part of me wondered if I was doing the right thing, but I shushed it.

"Avi here, Minnie? Nice fairy stay with me. She so nice!"

Her deep blue eyes were still full of the light of the sky, but her words made the hairs on my arms stand on end. "Fairy here, Avi?" I asked. I was starting to sound like her. "Stay with her and I'll be right back, okay?"

She nodded, but after glancing around, at the room full of boxes and shadows, she shook her head. "No, Minnie. I go, too."

"No, no, no." I stopped myself at the look of fear in her face. In a desperate move, I took Kota's gold coin out of my pocket and gave it to her. "Hold this. Sing 'Bah, Bah, Black Sheep' three times, and I'll be here before you know it."

Before she realized what I was doing, I dashed out. "I'll be right back," I called over my shoulder.

☀ ☀ ☀

I made it to first period, homeroom, right before roll call. Once Mr. Beck called my name and marked me as present, I raised my hand.

"May I go to the bathroom?" I asked. "I'm not feeling well."

He looked at me for a long moment. "Literally?" he asked, whatever that meant.

I was trembling, literally, in every sense of the word. I was like the last leaf hanging on to a tree during a storm. I was Jell-O during an earthquake.

Maybe the worry about my sister and my lack of real food the last few days was making me sick for real. The teacher must have seen something because he said, "Okay, and if after the bathroom you don't feel well, go to the office."

Never in all my years of school had I called home sick, not even when I had the stomach flu. I knew that even if I threw up all over the whole school and myself, Mamá couldn't leave her job, so I made myself hold up on the vomiting and fevering until I was safely home.

I dashed out of the room.

"Diarrhea, Miranda?" Canyon Smith asked.

It was a stupid joke and most of the people who heard him laughed. But the teacher was all like, "Literally, stop being so crude, Smith!"

Even if I knew he was only joking, I felt good that a teacher would tell off one of his favorites.

Once in the bathroom, I waited a few seconds before sneaking out again. Right as I was walking out to the office, I came across Mrs. Santos.

I almost turned back, but she'd seen me. If I turned around, she would think I was ignoring her because of the stupid play, as if I cared about the play now when my sister was all alone in the school.

"Minerva," she said. "Are you okay?"

Trying not to roll my eyes and groan took a lot more effort than I'd expected, so I made myself say, "I was actually on my way to the office. I'm not feeling well."

Mrs. Santos's face crumpled in sympathy.

"Pobrecita," she said in an accent different from the Argentine one I was used to, but I still understood. "Let me walk you then. In fact, I'll wait in the office with you. I'd like to talk with your mom when she comes to pick you up. Maybe we can talk about revising the play."

She kept talking, leading me by the arm, oblivious to the fact I was freaking out. How in the world was I going to get out of this? I didn't have time to waste. Anytime now, the loudspeaker would come on asking who'd left a baby in an out-of-the-way room, and then I'd be doomed.

"Minerva," Mrs. Santos said. "Have you read the book?"

I clenched my fists inside my sweatshirt kangaroo pocket. "Book? What book?" Who cared about books? I wanted to run.

"Are you okay, mi niña?" Mrs. Santos asked and stopped in the hallway to look at me straight in the eyes, right by the eighth-grade classroom, the one with the windows that oversaw the whole school.

I avoided her searching gaze so she wouldn't see how her "mi niña" had shaken me. I hadn't been anyone's little girl in a long time.

Maverick worked on an equation on the whiteboard inside the classroom. He'd made a mistake when he cancelled the factors. I wish I could tell him. I'd give anything to switch places with him. What would it be like if the biggest problem in your life could be solved with math?

"I'm sorry, Mrs. Santos. What book were you talking about?" I asked when Maverick looked in my direction and raised his eyebrows in question.

"*Peter Pan*. What else?" she said. "In the book, Tiger Lily is a warrior. You seem like a warrior. That's why I chose you, not because of your skin color."

We'd reached the office by now. I wanted this

woman to leave me alone once and for all. What did she know about warriors? She had no idea what my life was like.

As she had no idea that following me into the office was a disaster.

"Can I call home? I feel sick," I told the secretary.

"Oh, my goodness! The whole school is coming down with something," she exclaimed.

I didn't see anyone else waiting to go home. Either she was exaggerating, or she was talking about invisible students.

I needed to check on the baby. I had to get out.

The secretary handed me the phone, and after our hands accidentally brushed, she applied enough hand sanitizer to stop the black plague.

I dialed our home number. It rang and rang and no one picked up, of course. If it had, I might have had a major crisis—a happy one, but still.

"No one home?" the secretary asked after a few seconds.

I studied her face. She had beautiful skin, pale and smooth, and a dimple on her cheek even when she wasn't smiling.

"No, my mom's home with my sister. Maybe they stepped outside for a second," I said. "I'll try again."

She went back to her papers, and Mrs. Santos made copies next to the giant printer.

The phone rang until our answering machine picked up. At the sound of Mamá's voice asking me to leave a message, I got all teary and my throat hurt worse than when I had strep throat in third grade.

"Mamá, I need you," I said cupping my hand around the receiver so no one could hear me. "Please come to the school now."

I hung up and stood by the phone, hoping against hope, wishing for my mom to magically appear. But magic wasn't real. Things didn't happen just because we wanted them to—at least, not because *I* wanted them to.

"Go lie down in the nurse's office, sweetheart," the receptionist said to me, and then she looked behind me at Mrs. Santos, "My grandkids also get so emotional when they're sick. It's so sad and sweet."

The woman had curly short brown hair and a pretty flowery headband. She seemed too young to be a grandma, but then, I never had a grandma. I didn't know what they looked like.

When I turned to go to the nurse's office, I went around Mrs. Santos.

"Tell me when your mom gets here," she said. "I really want to talk with her."

She meant it in a nice way, I'm sure, but why couldn't she see how much worse she was making my life? If it weren't for her, I'd already be with my sister, my baby girl who was afraid of being alone.

"Don't cry, Minerva," she said softly, patting my shoulder.

I wasn't crying. I made such an effort not to shrug her hand away, I didn't have any energy left for her.

The nurse's office was just a regular room with a gray couch, a wooden chair, and a poster about *Vaccines! They save lives!* A bunch of children, each of a different race and color, ran toward a white guy dressed as a doctor as if he were a savior. In spite of my situation, I laughed softly before I let myself fall on the couch. My laughter threatened to turn into tears. The couch was mushy and comfortable, but worst-case scenarios with Avi as the sad protagonist popped up in my mind like horrible jack-in-the-box clowns. I sat up. I had to do something.

But what?

What?

I paced the room, trying to find anything that'd help me escape, but unless I pretended to be a walking poster, I came up with nothing. I placed my hand on the wall for support and landed on top of the fire emergency handle.

Fire emergency.

What would happen if I pulled it down? Last week we'd had a fire drill and the whole school had to evacuate the building. If I could get away after the office was evacuated, I could sneak out and no one would notice. Then if they called home, I could make something up.

First, I needed to shake off Mrs. Santos's hawk eyes, though.

Other than in the bathroom, privacy didn't exist here.

The bathroom.

"Excuse me," I said in such a sweet voice, Kota would be impressed. "I need to use the restroom. I think I'm going to be sick."

The receptionist's face of horror was so funny I almost smiled, and just in case, I put my hand over my mouth.

"Run, Minerva," the receptionist said shooing me away with her hands. "Run."

I didn't waste a second. I ran to the bathroom. When I reached it, I waited until my heart slowed down, but it wouldn't, so I didn't think twice. The fire handle was right next to the poster of a soldier telling students to WASH YOUR HANDS! KILL THE GERMS!

I pulled down the handle.

Chapter 10

The Grand Escape

THE ALARM BLARED so loud and shrill I was afraid my ears would bleed. I covered them and cowered in a corner of the bathroom to calm my shaking. But I had no time to lose. If I, who pulled the handle on purpose and knew exactly what would happen, was scared by the stupid alarm, Avi must be beside herself with terror.

I peeked out of the bathroom just in time to see people filing out of the classrooms obediently following their teachers. The office lady and Miss Santos marched ahead too, toward the exit.

I counted to three and ran in the opposite direction of the stream of students.

A hand grabbed my arm, and it whipped me to a stop. "You're going the wrong way!" Maverick yelled, but I could barely hear his voice above the racket of the alarm.

How long did I have until I lost my cover? I had to get to Avi.

I shrugged his hand away. "I'll tell you later!"

I ran away before he asked for an explanation, before the people around him surrounded me too, before a teacher could come up and stop me and send me to jail for wasting the city's resources.

I ran and ran, and when I reached the room where my sister was waiting, I stopped for a second to catch my breath.

"Avi!" I yelled, but I didn't even hear my own voice.

Trusting that no one would notice I was here, I turned the light on. Stars danced in my eyes.

Avi was nowhere. No hint of a barely three-year-old with caramel skin and blonde curly hair.

I frantically searched the room. Behind a pile of boxes, my sister slept with her thumb in her mouth and a trace of dried tears on her face.

If Kota were here, she would say, *"Minerva Soledad, what have you done? You've killed the baby!"*

Oh, my poor baby angel! My sweet Avi. My hand was cold on her warm forehead.

Breadcrumbs were scattered on the front of her shirt. I'd brought no food. What had she eaten? What if she found something poisoned in the basement and was now in a coma or something?

"Avi," I said, but the alarm still blared.

I picked her up. A sleeping baby weighs three times as much as an awake one. I had to use both arms to keep her from falling. Unable to switch off the light, I pushed the door with my hip and walked out to the fresh air and the warm sunshiny freedom.

The whole school was gathered on the sidewalk. Two fire engines and a crew of firemen were rushing into the school to quench a made-up fire. Such a scene! Mamá would ground me forever if she found out.

I don't know why I looked toward the auditorium when I did. Maybe I was subconsciously looking for a hiding place. But right then, I saw our stroller parked right next to a bike rack. The stroller I had left the night of the auditions! Someone must have moved it outside.

With no time to waste, I ran to it and placed my sister on it. She was breathing normally, and her hair was sweaty on the edge of her face. She sighed, blissfully unaware of the racket. Sometimes she would wake up if I moved in the bed at night. How come she was still asleep? This noise could have awakened the dead.

"Avi," I said, determined to make sure she was okay. "Avi."

Her eyes fluttered open. "Minnie," she whispered.

The ton of rocks on my shoulders dropped behind me. She was okay. She was still talking.

"Minnie, fairy nice. Cookie yummy." She closed her eyes and fell asleep again.

The wind blew my hair as a gray cloud covered the whole city. The first droplet fell smack on the middle of my forehead.

"Seriously?" I asked, although by now, I expected no answers from anyone.

Why wasn't anyone paying attention? No god or angels or fairies. I had to do it all on my own.

I walked to our house as fast as my legs let me. A stitch bit me on the side, and when I was about to stop to catch my breath, I saw a police car driving way slower than normal next to me on the sidewalk.

If the police stopped and asked me where I was going, what would I say? So much lying to the receptionist and Mrs. Santos left me out of excuses and inventions. The library was just ahead. If I sneaked in there, I could go online to look up that article about the play and send a message to my grandma while I was at it. I couldn't lead the police to our house. Kids my age were supposed to be at school.

What did the law do to truants? Truants who faked a fire to rescue their baby sister? Truants whose mom had been missing for days?

Biting my lip didn't bring any clarity. It wasn't until the police car drove away ahead of me that I realized I was hyperventilating.

Long breaths, Minerva. Calm down.

I looked over my shoulder, but no one followed me or even paid any attention to me. I ran to our house.

❋ ❋ ❋

Mr. Chang waved. "Hi there! Having a good day?" He worked in his yard, picking up apples, as I passed him.

Remembering Kota's advice, I briefly nodded. I couldn't even fake a smile. Now *I* was the silent sister. If he asked me what was happening, why all the emergency services were still zooming toward the school, I wouldn't be able to say anything but the truth.

My ears still throbbed. Would Avi's ears be hurt after being exposed to the noise for so long?

I held her close to me as I pulled her out of the stroller and walked down to our basement apartment. I'd get the stroller later. I always locked it, but now the door swung open when I barely touched it.

"I'm home!" I called, just in case Mamá was here waiting for me, in case miracles and magic really existed and my phone call had been heard and answered.

Of course the house was empty. No one was here. But someone had been inside. On the table was a gold coin.

The gold coin the Tooth Fairy had brought Kota, the one she'd wanted to take to school before I stopped her because she would lose it and then she would cry like La Llorona from Mamá's terrifying stories. The coin I'd given Avi so she could hold onto something familiar while I brought catastrophe on our heads.

The coin lay innocently on the table. The same one. *The* coin.

I was too tired to try to figure out the mystery. Too freaked out. I wanted to run out and ask for help. I wanted Mamá to get home already so this nightmare could become the past.

Instead of crying, *Where are my children?* like La Llorona, inside I was silently crying, *Where is my mother?* I needed to get a hold of my emotions, so I took a deep breath.

Avi slept while I went around the apartment searching every corner for someone who might be hiding, recording me as I freaked out. No one was there, which was good, but it didn't explain the mystery.

Avi woke up for lunch. Her body was a living clock. "Minnie? Cookies?"

She had little crumbs on the corner of her mouth. I know it was gross, but I had to know what she'd been eating. I wiped the crumbs off her face and put a tiny particle in my mouth. It *was* sweet like a cookie.

"Cookies, baby? Where did you get them?"

Avi looked at me for a few seconds, as if I were a curious beast she'd never seen before. She shrugged. "Fairy so nice, Minnie!"

"Fairies don't—"

I couldn't finish the sentence because she put a

tiny, pudgy finger on my lips. "Fairies nice, okay, Minnie? Everyfing okay."

Nothing was okay. Nothing, except that she seemed to be healthy and perfectly fine. Who was I to dash her hope and faith to pieces? I never had that kind of innocence, but why would I take it away from her?

"I don't have cookies," I said, "but I have my cupcake."

Her eyes lit up. I'd been saving it for when Mamá came home, but she might never. Someone might as well enjoy it before it went bad, and if it was an enchanted cupcake, then so what? My sister was an angel and she deserved magical cupcakes.

After she ate, she asked for me to put on *Chespirito* on the TV. I sat next to her through I don't know how many episodes, watching El Chavo and La Chilindrina hitting each other, and Doña Florinda slapping Don Ramón. How happy they were in the vecindad. El Chavo, the one that lived in a barrel, had no siblings. He had no one.

I was luckier than him. I had my girls. I would never let anyone take them away from me.

A knock on the door woke me up. Avi shook me softly. "Minnie, door."

Startled, I jumped off the couch. What time was it? Was I late to pick up Kota? Was it the police coming to get me for making a scene?

I didn't voice any of these questions, but I looked at Avi as if she could read my mind.

"Kota and Mavvy, Minnie," Avi said, pointing at the door.

"Are you a psychic or something?" I asked, unable to keep the edge off my words. But Avi was tough. Unlike Kota, she didn't get offended. She just pointed at the door again, like a miniature queen. I had no choice but to obey.

Another knock, and I braced myself for the worst (a police officer with handcuffs) and opened the door.

Chapter 11

Neverland

TRUE TO AVI'S words, Kota and Maverick—Mavvy?—
stood there holding hands like best friends.

"What are you doing here?" I asked. I know I
sounded like a jerk, but I could really not take any
more problems in my life, and him being at our house
was a huge problem. What had Kota told him?

"Don't look so shocked, Minerva Soledad," she
said, brushing against me as she walked into the house.
"I was tired of waiting, and when Maverick asked if
I needed anything, I asked in return, and I received."

Ask and ye shall receive.

Mamá loved this saying that she never practiced.
She never asked for anything: permission, help, or
forgiveness.

Good for me that Kota paid more attention to
words than actions.

"Maverick, thanks, but now is not a good moment for you to come in. We have a crisis," I said.

I leveled my eyes on him. He was so serious, I thought the whole world fit into his dark brown eyes. He'd walked Kota home, but he couldn't help us in any other way. He was just a kid, a year older than me in age but the seventh child, an only boy in a family of girls. I didn't have a lot of experience with people like him, but as far as I knew, it sounded like his life was pretty magical. How could he ever help and not treat us with pity?

No. Way.

"I saw you sneaking out of the school with your little sister. Can I come in?" he said, putting a hand on the doorframe.

If I slammed the door shut, I'd smash his fingers. And for the love of fairies, I wanted no more trouble. I didn't want to hurt him or for him to hate me. But he couldn't know.

Mr. Chang's head was barely visible from where I stood at the open door. Our neighbor and landlord was studying Maverick and me. What did he see? Did it look like I was letting friends in without permission? Would he complain to anyone?

I couldn't risk Mr. Chang coming over to check

on us and discover the rent-paying person was MIA.

I clenched my teeth to swallow an exclamation not proper for my sisters' ears and mumbled, "Okay, come in. But just for a second. And only because the landlord is looking at us suspiciously. Don't look!"

The dork was turning his head to see for himself if Mr. Chang was there. I had told him not to look. Why didn't he just do as I asked him?

Before I could change my mind and send him flying, Maverick stepped into our house and Kota slammed the door.

As if she had been waiting for him to cross into the threshold of our home before she could show her excitement, Avi ran to Maverick. "Mav," Avi said, "fairies so nice!"

Maverick laughed, bringing a little light to our shadowy apartment. Everything seemed clean—I really tried to keep things tidy—but I wondered what kind of home Maverick had. Did he notice the frayed curtains? The faded pillows on the sofa?

The more I dawdled, the more he'd notice how poor we were. I went straight to the heart of the problem. "You didn't see me sneak out of the school. I walked out in plain view of everyone. I had permission."

Not that I would add whose, but that was none of his business.

My main priority was to protect my sisters. I barely knew this guy. What if he went babbling our story to his parents or another kind of nosy grownup? We'd be doomed.

Maverick narrowed his eyes, like a kid watching a magician at the mall trying to figure out the trick. Why?

Kota. She had to go and babble to a stranger! When I got rid of him, I'd give her an earful she wouldn't forget any time soon. "What did you tell him, Kota?" I asked, sounding like an ogre.

She took a step back toward Maverick, her new protector. Her face turned bright red.

Maverick placed a hand on Kota's shoulder, like grownups sometimes do when they mean, *I got this, kid*. "She told me your mom's on a business trip and the babysitter didn't show up." He put out his other hand up like he was taking the presidential oath. "I promised I wouldn't tell anyone. My lips are sealed."

Kota looked at me with imploring eyes. Her lie was pretty convincing because she'd mixed in a little bit of the truth. Good job, Kota.

A war ranged inside me. I sat down on the couch, and Kota and Maverick joined me.

Maverick believed her. He had to be the most gullible boy in the world. Oh well, why not? Nothing fresh came to my mind. Maybe my reservoir of lies had gone dry with the imaginary fire.

"So you know?" I said. "You see? Our mom? She'll be back tonight."

"Tonight?" Avi's face lit up like Fourth of July fireworks.

Okay, so I didn't see that coming. It was too late to backtrack though. I either betrayed Mamá and made her look like the worst mother in the world, or I broke Avi's heart. Why did I always have to do the hardest things?

Kota bit her lip, and my insides twisted for her. She was trying so hard not to show Maverick the truth. So hard.

I kept my eyes on Maverick because I couldn't face Avi. I just couldn't. "She'll be back tonight."

"Okay," he said. "Kota said you took Avi to school. What happened? There was a fire in the teacher's lounge. They said a coffee maker started smoking and by the time the firemen showed up, the fire had spread to a curtain nearby."

Good thing I was already sitting, or I would have fainted right then. "Really?" My mind reeled. "Was anyone hurt?"

Maverick raked his hands through his hair. "No. The fire alarm saved everyone."

"The fire alarm? It saved everyone?" I knew I sounded so silly, repeating everything, but Maverick went on with the tale.

"The weird thing is that the alarm went off in the bathroom. It was a miracle, because the one in the break room wasn't working. The firemen said the batteries hadn't been changed in a while. Everyone's okay."

A real fire. And my sister had been in the school. If I hadn't slipped away. If I hadn't reached her in time. . . .

You saved everyone's lives, though, another voice said in my head.

It might have been right, but if something had happened to my sister, I would never forgive myself.

"What happened then?" I asked.

Kota and Avi's eyes went from me to Maverick as if they were watching a tennis match.

"All the parents were freaked out. There's no school for the rest of the week because they're checking each smoke detector and fire alarm in the building. It's all over the news."

"No school for the rest of the week?" Kota repeated, jumping off the chair and running to my arms, in her first spontaneous hug in like forever. "I'm so happy. Problem solved for now," she whispered in my ear.

"Fairy smart," Avi said in her clear bell-like voice.

Kota and I laughed and laughed, but it was just that we were so nervous about the whole situation. Maverick must have thought we were the weirdest girls he'd ever met.

"Okay, so we have to wait until your mom gets home?" Maverick asked, shattering the bubble of relief we had now that school wasn't a problem, at least until Monday.

Because by the way he'd propped his feet on the table, it looked like he wanted to stay waiting with us until Mamá came back, and that wasn't happening.

"Our mom comes back tonight. You can't be here when she arrives. She doesn't like friends over when she's not here."

Avi made a rolling-eyes kind of face that almost made me chuckle and ruin the authority in my voice

I'd managed so far. Mamá *never* let friends come over. Period. But I wasn't about to let Maverick know.

"Let's go to my house," Maverick said. "My mom's making a big dinner for my sister and her friends from church. It'll be fun."

"Okay," I said. I don't know what got into me. Maybe the fact that he'd mentioned dinner. One less thing to worry about. He'd also said his sister had invited friends. We wouldn't be the only ones there for the food.

"Really, Minnie? We go, Minnie?" Avi asked, clasping her hands like in prayer.

Just to make her happy, I said to Maverick, "But don't tell your parents our mom comes home tonight, or that I took my sister to school. It's not a secret, but my mom would be so embarrassed if anyone knew the babysitter didn't show up."

Mamá would be *so* embarrassed if she knew we were eating at people's house. That was the honest truth.

"I won't say anything," Maverick said. "But my mom won't judge. She goes out of town sometimes, too, and my sister babysits all the time."

I had a feeling his situation wasn't the same as ours. At all.

"Do you live very far?" I asked as my sisters put their jackets on without being told.

"Nope. We can go on my scooter."

"Scooter?" I asked. "How in the world would the four of us fit on a scooter?"

I was visualizing the skateboard with a handle, him being the skater boy and all, but right then, Kota clasped her hands and looked up to the ceiling in ecstasy. "Wait until you see his mini-motorcycle! It's the best!"

☀ ☀ ☀

Maverick's mini-motorcycle was a real motorcycle. He called it a scooter, but it was a battery-operated not-so-fast motorcycle that was a beauty all the same. I'd only ever seen them in television ads on Saturday mornings.

"Are you allowed to drive this without a license?" I asked, eyeing the scooter as if it were a spaceship.

Avi, already sitting very still on the scooter as Maverick put a helmet on her, gave me the thumbs up.

"It's a toy. Sorry, I only have one helmet," Maverick said.

Just a toy? My toys never looked anything like this.

"It's okay if Avi wears it," Kota chimed in, as if she had any say at all in what was okay and what wasn't. "I already wore it when he gave me a ride home."

"You rode this home?" My mom would ground me forever if she found out. She would be so furious she wouldn't talk to me until I was already the president of the US and gave her a special award for the most patient mom in the world.

"We can't all ride this," I said, trying to get between Maverick and Avi. "None of us can. It's too dangerous."

My sisters pouted and protested, but how could I let them? How could I?

Maverick scratched his head as he thought and thought. He looked like Winnie the Pooh. Adorable, but so clueless. "You're right."

"Minerva, why do you have to ruin all the fun?" Kota exclaimed, stomping her foot as if she were squashing me—a cockroach—under her pink tennis shoes.

"No, she's right," Maverick said, "Maybe you and Avi can sit on the scooter, and Minnie and I will walk beside you."

It was a perfectly reasonable solution. Then why did my heart feel like I'd missed out on a ride to the moon? The little ones perched on the motorcycle like queens.

The afternoon's breeze had a bite with the promise of fall already on the way. It blew my hair all over the place, like it wanted to get rid of my pitiful thoughts. How could I be jealous of my girls having a little fun?

Just then, a police car drove by, making my heart do all the somersaults and pirouettes I never allowed the girls to try. The cop was a bald guy with a reddish mustache. He looked like he was bored. Of course he would stop us.

Maverick waved at him, and the guy drove by, making a sign from his eyes to me that I interpreted like, *"I'm watching you."*

I shivered.

"Are you cold?" Maverick asked. "We're almost there."

I shook my head. He hadn't seen the guy's warning. It was so creepy I wanted to pretend it hadn't happened, so I listened quietly to my sisters' game of princesses flying in a magical ship guided by their noble servant Sir Maverick.

They never named me. I guess there was no room for me in their make-believe story, but I was grateful for something to keep me distracted from the cop and his warning.

"Their imaginations are so amazing!" Maverick said. "Kota was telling me all about the magic cupcakes and the golden coin she got for her lost tooth."

He gave me a look of *let's play along* that kind of annoyed me. Why did he believe the lies about our mom, but when we told the truth about the fairies, he didn't?

"Fairy's so nice, Mav," Avi said in a such a funny voice that Maverick and I exploded in laughter.

The trees' golden leaves fell on us like rain and then crunched under our feet.

"The fairy *is* nice, Avi," Kota said, like she was the expert. "Let them laugh, but if you don't believe, the Peques don't leave you presents. That's why Minerva doesn't get gold coins for her teeth."

Maverick looked at me again, his lips clamped down like he was suppressing laughter, but I didn't feel like laughing at all. Maybe my sister was right. But I believed now. How wouldn't I after seeing the golden coin on the table? I knew for a fact I had left it behind at the school. And what about those cupcakes? No, I believed. Why didn't I get any special favors from the Peques, then? Why wasn't Mamá back?

We walked along the street, up and up the hill to where the houses turned gigantic. We crossed the park with the splash pad—we'd been there once with Mamá when it was still summer and we were still happy.

This was such a nice area that it looked like after crossing my street, we'd traveled to a different world. My sisters felt the change too because they'd fallen quiet, in awe at the beautiful, enormous houses and lawns we passed.

Maverick stopped by the biggest house we'd seen yet. Life-sized bronze statues dotted the lawn. They looked tiny next to the house.

"Here we are. Welcome to my home."

Chapter 12

Fun and Games

THE GIRLS AND I walked into Maverick's house with the same kind of reverence one feels when entering a church or the library. Some kind of special, sacred place like that. But then, people didn't live in a church or a library, and in Maverick's house, it was obvious that in spite of the beauty and luxury, people lived here, in this castle, this mansion.

Maverick's sisters must have been off-the-charts popular girls. When Maverick said they'd invited a few friends from church, I imagined they'd have one or two friends each that they would read the Bible with, or something along those lines. But as soon as we walked in, a sea of every kind of fancy footwear received us at the front door. If I sold these shoes by the road, I'd make a fortune.

"Shoes off, Mavvy?" Avi asked, already kicking

off her boots, the ones Mamá had brought for her that last night.

In no shape or form would I take my shoes off. My socks weren't pretty, and I didn't want to leave my ugly no-name shoes next to all the nice ones. How to say this aloud though? While Maverick helped Avi and Kota with their shoes, I drifted away, looking at the beautiful family portraits on the walls. They'd been professionally made, at different locations, all exotic and faraway like the moon. At least for me, who'd never even been to the beach or Disneyland.

Maverick's family was so good-looking. They should all be on magazine covers. I recognized his mom as the lady who'd grabbed him by the arm the night of the auditions. She was as tall as his father. They both had short, dark hair that curled around their ears. They were perfectly matched. Her mouth was wide, perfect for smiling, which it looked like she did often.

Five of Maverick's sisters were smaller versions of their parents. Well-dressed, good-looking, happy. Even Maverick, who was Latino, and one of the sisters, who looked Asian and was obviously adopted too, had the same satisfied smile that said, *We have the greatest family on earth.*

"Maverick, are these your little friends?" asked a rich voice, the voice of a singer.

And there she was, Maverick's mom, in person and full color. She wore bright red high heels, inside the house.

Maverick's mom rocked.

She had wrinkles around her eyes and mouth, and after seeing her for two seconds, I could tell they were laugh and smile wrinkles. The marks of happiness, so opposite to the creases on Mamá's forehead from all her worrying.

"Welcome to our house," she said.

Apparently, I wasn't the only one who'd fallen for her at first sight. Avi ran and gave her a hug.

"Avi," Kota muttered, voicing the embarrassment (or jealousy) eating me from the inside out. "What are you doing?"

Mamá had been gone for three days, and Avi already was willing to go to anyone who showed her a little kindness. Was she forgetting Mamá already?

"Aren't you a sweetheart?" Maverick's mom said, hugging Avi back. "There's plenty of food, girls. Help yourselves while I sort out this crowd, okay?"

Avi ignored her instructions about the food and trailed behind her like a kite tail instead.

"These your friends, Mav?" Maverick's Asian sister asked. A group of friends followed her, and they all cooed and ahhed at Avi's angelic beauty. Even Kota's cheeks got kisses and pinches.

"I'm McKenna. Come play with us on the trampoline!" Maverick's sister said, and before I could blink, Kota was gone. Gone. She'd left me for the cool older girls, and I couldn't even blame her. I was too self-conscious of my clothes and the rest of my appearance to join them, but Kota didn't mind. She wanted to be someone's pet. Avi was still following Maverick's mom like a stray kitten that's been offered food and love. That left me free to hang out with my friend for the first time in forever.

"Looks like they left you all alone," Maverick joked.

He didn't know how liberating it was to be alone for a few minutes. First time I didn't have to worry about my sisters since they were born.

"Let's go eat," he said, and then he led me to the kitchen.

Good heavens and everything good on earth! The kitchen was a dream. I'd never seen anything like it before. The stainless-steel appliances gleamed against the blackness of the stone countertops, so huge that they held trays and trays of food and still there was room to sit beside them on stools that looked straight out of a catalog. I was sure they were.

Seeing so much food in one place made me dizzy.

"Try a slider," Maverick said, passing a tray of mini-burgers in my direction.

I eyed them with love and took one, although I wanted to grab the whole tray and run away before they disappeared. This had to be a fantasy. The bread and meat melted in my mouth. Flavors exploded on my tongue, and tears sprang to my eyes. Food was the best thing in the world.

From a corner of my eye, I saw Avi daintily eating a stick of fruits at the counter top, holding Maverick's mom's hand. The ordeal of leaving Avi in the school basement, the fire, and the whole morning seemed like a million years away.

If only I could bottle this moment forever. When we returned home, the house would still be empty, our mom gone. No food in the cupboards. Why couldn't we get a family like this?

Why did some have so much material stuff, so many people to love and care for them, and others had so little? Whoever was in charge of dividing the good things in life had seriously failed at long division.

"Aren't you hungry?" Maverick asked.

My plate was piled with food, but the one slider I'd eaten sat in my stomach like a stone. Not because I didn't want to eat—oh yes, I wanted to eat this delicious food—but the thought that the life I was given was so unfair killed my appetite.

As soon as it had come, I shooed the thought away. How wasn't I going to eat this amazing food? Rock in the pit of my stomach or not, I kept on chewing until it dissolved, and I moved on to another slider. It was even more delicious than the first.

"I'm just thinking," I replied, my eyes on Kota doing an impersonation of some YouTuber to make McKenna and her friends laugh, and being totally successful at it.

Ask and you shall receive, Kota had said.

My heart was a twisting bunny inside me. I couldn't hold this secret any longer. Someone else had to know.

"Maverick?" I said, avoiding his eyes because I was too embarrassed. "Can you keep a secret?"

☀ ☀ ☀

Maverick liked secrets.

He led me to a room he called the den, this

super-modern play area at the other end of the house, complete with real arcade games, ping-pong and foosball tables, and room to spare. In a corner, a canopy made the perfect secret-telling spot. We sat there.

"Go ahead," he said, probably confusing my shock at the size of his house with me changing my mind about revealing my secret.

I was stunned by the size of this place. My sisters and I could happily live in a little out-of-the-way corner, and no one would ever notice us. We'd be in no one's way.

Maverick was a good listener. He didn't interrupt as I told him everything. That is, everything but the part about the fairies and their help. Kota had already told him, and he hadn't believed it.

I hated to see the weight of my worry transferred to him like this, but so many people had helped him carry his burdens all his life. I didn't have anyone but him, and the weight of my secret was too much for me. I wanted out. I wanted peace.

"Are you serious? She just left?" he asked.

I fidgeted on my seat. "I don't know. I don't know what she did or what happened. I just know she didn't come back from work. It's been three full days. Since Sunday night."

He scratched his head. Maybe it was the worry, but his face went all pointy and serious, all the happiness gone from him. "We can tell my mom and ask her to help you. Once the people leave, we can see if you guys can sleep here. Until your mom comes back."

When I exhaled, my shoulders relaxed for the first time since Monday morning. "Really? Thank you!"

Maverick bit his lip and glanced out to the foosball table where another one of his sisters—Rose—laughed with some friends.

"Should we tell your mom right now, though? Maybe she can help me call her job and see if she left a message there or something." Now that I had told him my secret, I wondered why I'd kept it to myself for so long.

A cloud went over Maverick's face. "Let's wait until after the party. There are too many things going on right now."

He was totally right. The house was so huge, and more and more people showed up by the minute. Every once in a while, I checked on the girls, and every time, they were happy being someone's doll. So I ate the delicious food although I was already full, and waited.

I'd take Maverick's and his mom's help, but I

should also do something on my part, and the only person from my family I could ask for help was my unknown grandma.

"Do you have a computer?" I asked.

"Sure. What for?" Maverick's earlier excitement with me and my sisters' staying over was starting to go weak. I knew the signs: The too-ready answers. The faraway look in his eyes. In case us staying here was a no-go, we needed a plan B.

I told him about Abuela, and while I talked, he headed to one of the computers just sitting there on a table (there were five. Five computers) and clicked on the keyboard for a couple of minutes.

"Ta-da!" he finally said, and pointed to the picture of a lady on a screen. Fátima Grant, my abuela. Mamá's mother. I looked so much like her there was no question we were related. The same angular face. The same slender and small body frame.

"Wow," Maverick said. "She looks like she could be your mom. She's a young-looking grandma."

She was. Her hair was curly like mine, and her white smile was framed by bright-pink painted lips. She looked even younger than my mom, who never wore makeup.

"Do you think it's okay if I wrote her a message?"

"Of course! She can come help you maybe."

It wasn't so easy for a person to travel from the other end of the world, especially to see three girls she'd never met before. But she was the only one who could help.

I wrote in Spanish, knowing I would have tons of errors. I had never learned to spell in Spanish, but maybe she would understand me all the same.

Abuela,

This is Minerva, your daughter Natalia's daughter. Our mom is gone. We don't know where she is. We need help. Call us.

I added our phone number and address, hoping I was giving her all the information she'd need to contact me. I clicked send while my heart pounded up a storm.

If only it were this easy for a person to travel! Easy like sending a message on the internet. When was someone going to invent an instant-travel machine? When I was the president of the United States, I would hire the best scientists in the world to build it for kids who were lonely. For kids who'd never met their family from faraway places in the world.

"I'm going to the bathroom and I'll be right back, okay?" Maverick said, leaving me at the computers a little longer.

"Okay," I said, realizing this was the perfect opportunity to look up that article Mamá had once told me about. The one about the *Peter Pan* play.

The Internet is magic. A few clicks later, I'd found an article from the Smithsonian museum that explained how *Peter Pan* was so offensive to Indigenous people. Best of all, it included a section on how some directors had replaced the Indians with Amazons. There was another one from The Children's Theater Company website that explained how the play had been adapted for schools. I felt like shouting "Eureka!" Instead, I emailed the links to Mrs. Santos and printed out the articles to read again at home.

I grabbed the still-warm papers from the printer, folded them, and was putting them in my pocket when Maverick returned from the bathroom.

"What do you want to do now?" he asked. "I mean, before we tell my mom you guys are staying over."

Poor Maverick. He thought my problem would be solved so easily. But the more I looked around me, the more I noticed that we couldn't stay here. Sure, his mom could help me find my mom, ask around, but I knew three girls with no family was a bigger burden than anyone would like to deal with. Would I repay the Sorensens' kindness by bringing so many issues to them?

I wasn't such a bad friend to go that low, I hoped.

But I could have fun for a little while longer, before the slap of being alone woke me up to reality.

Kota and Avi had eaten their fill and were having fun. Avi played with another little girl her age who wore the most darling outfit ever. She looked like a princess in a pink silk dress and tiara. The two babies played with a ceramic tea set, their movements so dainty and careful my eyes prickled with emotion. Avi had never had a friend before.

Meanwhile, Kota was getting drunk on soda, watching a movie with the teenagers. It was still early.

My sisters were having fun.

Maybe *I* could have some fun.

"Can we go on a scooter ride?" I asked.

Maverick smiled like a devil. "You're not scared?"

I bit down on my lips, but I was sure he could tell I was smiling.

"Okay," he said. "I'll drive first so you can know

what it's like, how it works. There's no gears at all, just the go button and the brakes. It's easy enough."

Once outside, I sat behind him, and trying to touch as little of him as possible, I grabbed the edge of his shirt. The scooter lurched forward. Afraid I'd fall on my head, I grabbed the back of the seat.

"Okay back there?" he asked.

"Okay," I said, but what I really wanted to say was, *What did I get myself into?*

The sound of crunching leaves mixed with the buzzing of the engine as we zoomed through the neighborhood. If this was what flying felt like, then maybe Peter Pan wasn't such an idiot. Maybe it would be worth staying a kid forever for a chance to go zipping through the neighborhood like motorized mosquitos. Mosquitos were still flyers, and flying meant freedom.

My eyes watered because of the cold air, and soon my nose started running. Good thing I had wiped it with the back of my hand before Maverick noticed because when we went around a corner, Maverick stopped at a house even bigger and more beautiful than his. This house was majestic enough to be the mayor's house. Bailey's house? I wondered if she lived in this neighborhood. She had to.

"What are you doing?" I asked.

"This is Blessings's house," Maverick said. "I'll say hi. Do you mind?"

"No," I said in a tone that meant *I don't care at all,* but I cared. He'd been hanging out with me. Why did he need Blessings now?

Because I was jealous but not stupid, I couldn't tell my only friend that I wanted him to hang out only with me. How weird would that be? But a corner of my puppy heart wished that if I wasn't his only friend, then I was his best friend. Maybe when I ran for student body president, he could manage my campaign. Maverick knew all the right people.

"Can I go on a ride by myself while you hang out with him? Just a turn around the block," I said.

Maverick didn't even bat an eyelash. "Sure."

Then, thinking better of my idea, I asked, "I've never driven one before. Is it hard?"

Maverick laughed and shook his head. "It's just like riding a bicycle."

I didn't know how to ride a bike, either, but I didn't want him to know.

One day, people would ask, "President Miranda, how did you learn to ride your motorcycle?", and I would tell the story, and everyone would envy the wonderful friend I had. That's why Maverick would make an excellent campaign manager. The idea appealed to me more and more by the second.

He explained which buttons to push, how to stop, and to pay attention to the sound. "You'll notice how the intensity of the . . . I don't know what to call it . . . the *BROOM, BROOM* sound decreases."

"The thrum," I said, trying not to laugh. "The *BROOM, BROOM* sound is called *thrum*."

The streetlight came on in time to shine the surprise on his face. "Ooh! The thrum, huh?"

"See you later," I said, smiling so wide my cheeks hurt.

He waved his hand as he walked to Blessings's front door. Blessings? Understatement of the year. The guy was an All-In-One if there ever was one. Good looking, rich, well liked, star of the play.

I turned the engine on, and after a couple of deep breaths, I let go.

At first, the scooter wobbled, but I straightened it out before it leaned too much to the side. Still, sweat exploded in my armpits, but the wind quickly made the nerves go away. My knuckles shone white under the street lamps, but by the second lap, I let my hands relax a little.

I also dared to look at my surroundings. Not only were the houses enormous in this neighborhood, but the orchards extended over acres of land, waiting with open branches to hand out food that no one needed or even wanted. Apples lay on the ground unpicked. Maybe in the future, if we needed to, the girls and I could come to this area and take the unwanted food we needed so much.

The sound of the thrum changed when I passed Blessings's house the third time.

I should've stopped then.

But the night was beautiful, and I was alone and free. Nothing could go wrong.

Until the scooter stuttered, shivered, and stopped, right in a stretch of road where there were no street lamps and where the next house looked so far it might as well be in another world.

"Seriously?" I said, cursing myself for not noticing how late it was, how the purplish blue of the sky had turned into deep ink. Most importantly, for not paying attention to the sound of the thrum. The thrum!

A car zoomed by me and honked the horn so loud I had a flashback to the school alarm and how close I'd been to disaster. Mamá always said the fairies went to sleep when the sun went down. If that part of her tales was true, then I doubted anyone was coming to help me now.

I had to go get help, but I couldn't leave the scooter behind. What if it got stolen or a car ran it over? It was Maverick's and I had to take better care of it than if it were my own. So, I grabbed the handle and walked it uphill, pretending the shadows didn't scare me, that I didn't imagine a kidnapper hiding behind every tree. The scooter without power was heavier than when Maverick and I had walked my sisters to his house.

Like a baby, a sleeping scooter was much heavier than one that was awake.

A flash of red and blue lights behind me froze me in my tracks.

But it was at the sound of the voice that I started shivering, and not because I was cold. "Where are you going with that and where did you get it, young lady?" the bald police officer I'd seen several times before asked.

Chapter 13

Caught and Returned

*I*F I DROPPED the scooter and ran, I could hide among the trees and stay still as a shadow until the officer got tired and went away. But then he could stay here all night and find me with his laser-beam flashlight, and then what would I tell him, what excuse would I give him for running away? If he called for backup, I'd be in real trouble.

"Do you speak English?" he asked. "Where are you going, I said!"

Slowly, I turned around to face him. What I saw didn't reassure me. Not a tiny bit. His dark brown eyes didn't reflect any kindness.

Under other circumstances, I'd give him a very insolent answer, like: *Yes, I speak English and Spanish. Did you know bilingual people are smarter than those who only speak one language?*

I suspected he wouldn't react kindly to my cheekiness. Besides, I was tired of lying and running.

Maybe it was my time to face whatever the future sent me, and when I got there, I'd deal with whatever it brought: foster home for me and my sisters, a life apart from each other. Maybe if they were super lucky, they'd be placed with a nice family like Maverick's or Blessings's, and they wouldn't be hungry or alone anymore.

With nothing to hide, I faced the officer with my head held high like I thought a princess might. I'd done nothing wrong.

The officer's mouth quivered in a smile that made me shudder. "Where did you get this scooter? A neighbor a street over complained of some Mexican girls trying to steal vegetables and fruit from the co-op garden. Is that you? Are you and your friends stealing?"

Understanding fell on me like an anvil. It wasn't a community garden then. It was a co-op, the kind people have to pay for before they can take produce from it. We never intended to steal anything, but suddenly I saw things from the garden lady's perspective. We weren't Mexican, though. We were born in Utah.

"My friend let me ride his scooter," I said in a small, quivery voice.

The officer *tsk*ed and clicked his tongue as if I'd given the wrong answer. "I've been watching you all day. You either missed school or cut out of class right when the alarm went off. Did you have anything to do with that?"

The mask that usually hid my true emotions slipped off my face. That was the only explanation for the guy's expression. He smiled like he'd solved the crime of the century. "Aha! I knew you had something to do with that."

The officer stepped in my direction, and I raised my arms, I'm not sure why. Maybe to show him I wasn't armed. Right then, I saw Maverick and Blessings running in our direction, waving their hands in the air and yelling, "Minnie! Minnie! Are you okay?"

Maverick reached me first and hugged me so tight I had to make a superhuman effort not to start crying right then.

"What took you so long?" he asked. "I thought a car had run you over or something."

Blessings stood a little behind us, eyeing the officer with suspicion.

"So you were telling the truth about the scooter, then?" the officer's voice was little nicer now that my friends were with me. He must know that the boys were from this rich neighborhood.

"Of course she was telling the truth! What did you think?" Maverick exclaimed, outraged.

Oh, my dear Maverick. So spoiled. He didn't know when to shut his mouth and take it in silence.

"Don't talk back at me, kid," the officer hollered, making Maverick flinch. "In any case, it's late for kids your age to be out and about. How old are you, anyway? I'll drive you guys to your homes and have a word with your moms. It's always *your* kind making my life extra hard."

Our kind? What did he even mean?

My mind was going a billion miles an hour trying to figure out what to say. I needed to get Maverick and Blessings out of this mess. If it weren't for them, I would've fainted right then and there. How did I get myself into this situation? To go home in a police car would be the ultimate humiliation.

Blessings reacted first, keeping his hands visible. "I was just helping Maverick look for Minerva. I don't want to get in any trouble."

The officer was already putting the scooter in the

cruiser's trunk. "I want to make sure your moms know you're driving around with no helmets on."

My brain shriveled out of clever comebacks. Blessings hadn't done anything. Apparently, Maverick's smart-alecky attitude went missing too because he didn't say anything either.

Without a word, I got into the car and sat on my hands. What could I say once we arrived at my house? What would the cop say when he saw it was dark and empty? Would we continue to Maverick's and Blessings's? What about after they were safe and sound with their families? I didn't want to be last and be alone in the car with him.

The guy had other ideas though. "I know you live on Chrysanthemum Way, but I haven't figured out the house," he said.

Maverick and I exchanged a look of complete horror.

What else did the cop know? How long had he been following me? The ride was short, of course. I hadn't realized we were so close to my house or I would've made a run for it at as soon as I saw the lights.

Ay, Minerva! You were doing a good job staying off the radar, and then you had to go and ruin it!

"It's okay, Minnie," Maverick whispered. "It'll be okay."

He knew what this meant. He knew my mom wasn't home and then we would all be in so much trouble. There was nothing he could do to help me, though.

Mr. Chang's house was all lit up like there was a party. A stream of cars lined the street. I'd never seen even a single person visiting our landlord. Of course he had to have a party the night the police brought me home. I'd never live down this day.

"Here we are," I said, my voice choked with nerves.

The officer got out of the car and opened my door. So far, he was being a gentleman. I couldn't complain, but there was a dark, negative energy flowing from him that told me tonight wouldn't end on a happy note.

Maverick made as if to get out of the car, too.

"Not too fast, *amigo*," the cop said, stretching the word into an insult. "You and Big Eyes there stay put."

Blessing's eyes were normal size. The comment was beyond inappropriate. Why did this man feel it was okay to disrespect us? But what could *I* do?

I got out of the car and marched ahead, the officer following closely behind. The front door light was on, although I remembered clearly turning it off before we left for Maverick's today.

I should've stayed home all night.

Nothing good came of disobeying.

I'd be in so much trouble.

"My mom might not be home until later," I said, trying to come up with some excuse that would make my situation better. "She works late sometimes."

"How old are you? It's against the law for a minor your age to be alone for more than four hours in a twenty-four-hour period. If she's not home, then I'll wait outside until she comes back. Or better yet, I'll get my friends from Child and Family Services to come keep me company until she returns."

Okay, keep your mouth glued, Minerva. No more words.

The guy had a smile on his face as if he knew there was no mother at my house, as if he knew I was lying.

I stood under the porch light.

The bowl for the Peques' milk was empty. Glitter sparkled around it just like the stars. The mountains were magically beautiful with clouds swirling around them. Maybe they had some power to grant wishes. I wished with all my heart that the officer would forget why he was here and would go back to whatever police officers do when they're not following kids or trying to catch vegetable thieves.

He knocked on the door.

One.

Twice.

Three times.

Before he could knock a fourth time, and I could tell him there was no one home, the door opened.

Mamá, looking pale like she hadn't seen the sun in decades, stared at the police officer.

I screamed.

If I won a billion dollars in a lottery,

If I won the student body elections,

If I became the queen of Neverland,

I wouldn't have screamed a happier sound.

To Mamá's credit, she smiled. Kind of. Her eyes went crinkly in the corners and lost a little of that vicious glint she'd sent the officer.

"Mamá!" I hugged her, and she staggered back.

She wore an outfit I'd never seen before—jeans and a white blouse, all billowy and with curlicues embroidered on the hem. She smelled of a laundry detergent that wasn't the kind we used. Her clothes were new to her, but they weren't new, by any means. She was so cold, the cold seeped through the cotton fabric, and she shivered. But she was here, in the flesh.

"Mamá, estoy feliz!" I only managed to say because I didn't want to cry in front of the police officer.

He wasn't a happy camper. Maybe he got worried about what I said in Spanish. Lifting his hands, he said, "I don't know what she's telling you, but my only interest was to see to her safety and the boys'."

Maverick and Blessings watched us from the car. Blessings was totally oblivious to what Mamá's presence meant. Maverick, though, gave me the thumbs up, like he meant, "Perfect timing!"

Mamá turned businesslike and asked, "Was she in any trouble?" Her calm tone of voice invoked respect.

The officer cleared his throat and looked down to his feet. I looked, too. His shoes were scuffed on the points.

"Not exactly, ma'am. She was out riding a scooter without a helmet. We don't want her to fall and hurt that pretty head now, do we?"

We.

Mamá laughed, but I knew that little laugh. She wasn't amused. "Thank you for escorting my child to make sure she's okay. Now, how may I help you?"

I took Mamá's hand in mine. It was like holding an icicle. I looked to see it was really her hand and noticed she wore a white plastic bracelet, like the kind she kept in her box of memories. She'd worn something like this when Avi was born.

A hospital bracelet.

Under the tinge of detergent I smelled on her clothes, there was a whiff of disinfectant and medicine. Paper bags with pharmacy labels on them covered the kitchen table.

I had a million questions, but the officer kept saying tonterías to cover his backside.

"This street is so dark. And did you know there was a drug house in the neighborhood not too long ago? Yes, even in this nice neighborhood! We can never be too careful. Some ex-customers still don't want to understand it's not here anymore."

Mamá let him blabber on, and he finally agreed to leave the boys at our house under the condition that they would call their parents to pick them up. He left the scooter by the curb and he drove away, the lights of his cruiser off.

As soon as he was gone, Maverick said, "Mrs. Miranda, it's totally my fault. Minnie said she had to stay home because you'd be back from work, but I so wanted her to come to my house, and then I *convinced* her to ride my scooter and she *insisted* she needed a helmet, but then I went to Blessings's house and then I got distracted. And yeah, it's totally my fault." He was panting at the end, his freckles standing out against his face.

Stupid boy. She hated being called Mrs. Miranda, and for people to call me Minnie. The fact that I'd been persuaded to ride a scooter (which was a lie) would be evidence enough to ground me for the rest of my life. But it was proof of how sick she felt that she didn't say anything else; she didn't complain or even look at me in that way of hers of saying, "Ya vas a ver. When your friends leave, you'll see how mad I am at you."

Instead, Mamá brushed Maverick's head in a way that gave me shivers. "You're such a good friend. Thank you. Now, why don't you call your parents to pick you up? And Minerva?" She emphasized my name, which told me just because she hadn't protested didn't mean she'd start calling me by a diminutive now. "Where are your sisters?"

I cleared my throat and wrung my hands. Now I had it coming.

There was no point in delaying the inevitable, so I went with the truth. "They're at Maverick's, Mamá. There's a party there, and they were playing Barbies. I'll go get them."

She sat on the sofa, straight-backed but shaking. I suspected that if she leaned back, she wouldn't be able to leave her seat again, so I held her hand to let her know I'd get rid of my friends as fast as lightning, so she could stop pretending she was all right.

But she pressed my hand. "Stay," she said. "Maverick, can you call your parents and see if they could bring the girls when they come pick you up? The officer left, but I don't put it beyond him to lurk around to catch you in a mischief of some sort."

Blessings and Maverick exchanged a look. Even they could tell she wasn't well.

"For sure," Maverick said.

We sat in silence. I had so many questions in my mind for my mom, I didn't know where to start. Maverick and Blessings were whispering, and Mamá kept her eyes closed as if she were praying.

"Are you okay, Mamá?" I asked. "I'll make you a cup of tea."

It'd have to be sugarless because we had run out this morning and with the whole disturbance at school, I hadn't been able to snatch a few packets from the lunchroom to bring home.

She didn't say anything, though. Her breathing was shallow and fast. I rushed to make her a tea, anything to make her feel better.

After calling his mom on his cell phone, Maverick followed me to the kitchen. "Is your mom okay? She looks really sick."

Oh, Maverick. He wasn't so clueless after all.

Chapter 14

The Quest Home

"SHE'LL BE FINE," I said, surprising myself with the calmness of my voice. "She just needs to rest. It must be her blood sugar. Sometimes it's low."

I don't know if Maverick believed me, but before he could say anything else, someone knocked on the door. I ran to open it, but the door flew open and pushed me out of the way. Kota ran into the house like a tornado.

"Mamá!" she cried and threw herself onto our mother like I would've wanted but wasn't brave enough to do.

My sister's sobs broke my heart.

Mamá, maybe sensing that Maverick's parents were close behind, gently pushed Kota away, and in the sweetest voice I'd ever heard her use, she said, "Calm down, mi amor. After the company leaves, you can cry all you want."

Kota understood in an instant. Her tears seemed to run back into her eyes. They dried like *this*. She hiccupped once, but soon her breathing went back to normal. Her eyes though stayed swollen and her face splotchy.

"Go wash your face in the bathroom and wait until I ask you to come out," Mamá instructed.

Maverick seemed to get cleverer by the second. He took in the whole situation and his face changed, like he understood what was really going on. He walked out to the front door in time to intercept his mom from coming into our house. Mamá struggled to get back on her feet, and she finally did in time to receive the visitors.

Mrs. Sorensen carried a sleeping Avi in her arms. "Well, hello! So nice to finally meet you! My Maverick's enchanted by your girls!"

"Mom!" he exclaimed. "What are you even saying?"

I avoided looking him in the eyes to save his ego. And mine.

"Let's go to the car, Blessings," he said. "Let's go,

Mom. Mrs. Miranda just came home from work."

I cringed on Mamá's behalf now. I knew what he was trying to do, but now Mamá looked like the kind of person that would go to work all day and leave her kids alone. Which she did, but no one would understand why.

We didn't need Maverick's excuses. We could totally take care of ourselves. That's exactly what we'd been doing since Papá walked out.

Mrs. Sorensen shrugged. "I'm sorry, son. I forget how embarrassing moms can be sometimes."

She made a face like expecting Mamá would agree, but my poor mother swayed in place, and to disguise her dizziness, she held onto my shoulder. She pressed once, and I understood immediately what she wanted me to do.

"Thanks for bringing my sister, Mrs. Sorensen. I'll have her, please."

Mrs. Sorensen looked surprised, but she handed me the sleeping baby. "They're such sweethearts! I wanted to keep them all, especially this treasure. She talked up a storm tonight. She must have made herself tired, with all the telling stories about fairies and magic coins. According to her, there's a dungeon at the middle school!"

She laughed, but my hairs stood on end in alarm. Mamá's face also got startled at the mention of Avi's talking.

On my way to the bedroom, I smiled at her briefly, hoping she'd understand that I meant for her to wait until I could explain. She nodded so imperceptibly, only I could tell she had understood.

Avi nestled in the bed when I put her down, and I covered her with her Winnie the Pooh blanket. By the time I came back to the kitchen with the blanket Mrs. Sorensen had brought her in, Mamá was curled up in the couch, but looking at me with a smile on her face.

I ran to hug her, but she put a hand up to stop me. "My stomach hurts a lot. Disculpa, mi amor. I don't mean to put you off, but I'm hurting really bad."

I made as if to follow Mrs. Sorensen out. From the window, I saw all of them walking toward their car.

"She says Avi can keep the blanket," Mamá whispered.

I was glad Mrs. Sorensen hadn't stayed talking, but I wished I could've said goodnight to Maverick. He must have thought we were a bunch of ungrateful girls.

"What happened to you, Mamá?" I asked, brushing her hair out of her face. Her skin felt clammy to the touch.

Mamá grimaced and clutched at her stomach. "Give me a minute. I took my medicine right before you got home. It should take effect any moment now."

I sat beside her, holding her hand. It was so surreal to have her sitting next to me. Looking back, it seemed like the last few days had been a nightmare, and I was finally waking up. From now on though, life would continue as usual, as normal.

A muffled voice broke the charged silence of the kitchen. "Can I come out now, Mamá?"

I laughed in spite of myself. Silly Kota. Was she still in the bathroom waiting?

I didn't want Avi to wake up, and I wanted to warn Kota that Mamá was sick, so I tiptoed to the bathroom. "Careful when you hug her. She's sick."

Kota nodded once, and we went back to the living room hand in hand.

Mamá watched us with a smile on her face that wasn't enough to cover the pain she must have been in. She had more color in her face, and her hands were still cold but felt alive.

"What happened?" Kota asked. "Where were you, Mamá? We missed you so much! It was so hard to live without you!"

Kota's tears streamed down her face. But I held

mine in. Two crying girls was too much work for Mamá. She didn't look like she could deal with a lot of emotions right now.

"I'll tell you the whole thing if you promise to be strong a little bit longer." I only heard her because I held my breath to catch her every word. "The medicine I took takes the pain away, but it also makes me tired. If . . . if I . . . if I drift off before I finish . . . don't wake me up. I'll tell you more tomorrow."

"Of course," I said before Kota could argue. "Okay, Kota? Let's sit here on the floor," I said, patting the carpet. It felt like we were getting ready for a fairy story. This one had a happy ending, because she was here now.

Mamá spoke again. "That night I went to work, I fainted in the street after I got off the bus and woke up hours later in a hospital."

Kota looked at me, her eyes and mouth in an expression of total horror. I pressed her hand to let her know everything would be okay. Wasn't Mamá with us now? Kota nodded at me, letting me know she'd gotten the message.

Mamá's eyes were closed, and she spoke in a whisper that gave me goosebumps. "The whole time I had these dreams that I was flying to Neverland, but I wanted to come home. One time I woke up, but the doctors wouldn't let me leave the bed yet. I couldn't really get up on my own. Not even to follow the fairy lights. . . ."

She and I sighed at the same time. I didn't know why she did, but my sigh was born of frustration. Fairies? Did fairies really try to help her come home? I didn't want to interrupt her, so I let her continue.

"This morning, though, I told them I was ready to come home with you, my sweet princesas. So . . . they let me go. . . ."

She sighed at the end, and then her breathing turned slower and slower until I realized she was asleep.

Kota and I looked at each other in silence. I motioned for her to wait for me in the kitchen.

"I'll make the mátes," she mouthed.

"I'll take care of the water," I said, and she nodded wordlessly.

I covered Mamá with her blanket, the one I was keeping on my bed every night to pretend she was with me, hugging me when it was dark.

"Mamá," I whispered, caressing her head. It looked greasy and unkempt, like she hadn't even brushed it in a long time, but her hands were tinged with golden glitter, the kind I'd been finding all over our house. I didn't know what to think anymore. "Thanks for coming back. Te quiero, Mamá." Just in case, I whispered, "Thanks for bringing her home, Peques."

When she slept, her mouth pouted the same way as Kota's. I wanted to hug my mamá and pass on my strength to her, but I didn't want to bother her. I went back to the kitchen where Kota had made the yerba máte tea. Mamá had often told us not to waste her yerba, but I needed a little bit of comfort, and sometimes when Mamá and I talked late into the night, she would let me have máte with her. Mamá had never let me boil the water before, but in the last few days, I'd proved I could do this simple thing without getting hurt.

Carefully, I heated the water and took the presiding place at the table. My sister didn't complain because she knew the rules. The oldest serves the máte and passes it around.

"She doesn't look that well," Kota said, stating the obvious.

"But she's home. She can get better if we're good, you know? We just need to be really good and a lot of help so she can recover."

In the end, Kota and I drank máte in silence, at peace that Mamá was home, but feeling the future looming in front of us. We'd barely survived these last three days, but what would we do from now on? Rent was due soon, and if Mamá hadn't worked, all the money we had was what I had found in her wallet in her closet.

"It's so late, and I'm so tired!" Kota said, yawning widely.

"Let's go to sleep," I finally said.

In the darkness of the night, I woke up to the sound of Mamá when she got up to throw up and cry silently.

Chapter 15

The Twice-Over Mother

*K*OTA DIDN'T WANT to go to school.

"You have to," I said. "We need to help Mamá. I told you last night and you were perfectly fine with the plan. Besides, if you go to school, you'll get to eat lunch. We don't have a lot of food here."

That woke her up in every sense of the word.

I walked her to school and hurried back home to Mamá and Avi, who was still sleeping and hadn't moved since the night before. It worried me how much Avi slept. Was that normal? Was it because she was growing? Was it because she'd been so hungry? Maybe I'd take a book out of the library to read up on normal toddler behavior.

Good thing *I* didn't have school, so while Mamá showered (she said she hadn't had a proper shower since the night she left for work and we'd seen her for the last time), I straightened up the room and made toast and tea for her.

"Thank you, mi amor," she said.

But the tea went cold, and the toast rested untouched on the plate.

Avi toddled into the room, rubbing her eyes like she wasn't sure where she was. Poor thing, she'd gone to bed in a mansion and woken up in our run-down apartment. What was she thinking?

When she saw Mamá, she looked at me and ran into my arms. "Mami, Minnie? That Mami?" she whispered only for my ears, her tiny arms clutching me so hard that I had a hard time breathing.

Mamá, who hadn't cried when the police officer brought me home, who'd held herself stoic like a queen when Mrs. Sorensen came over, who had told us her tale of horror dry-eyed, burst into tears.

"Is she talking? Avalon? Say hi to Mami?"

Avalon shook her head.

"Why, Avi?" I said. "Say hi to Mamá. Aren't you happy she's back?"

Avalon didn't know how to lie yet. Her thoughts and feelings were plain on her face. Just in case her look of disdain wasn't enough, she pointed at Mamá and said, "Mean Mamá. Avi so sad."

My sisters had mastered the art of expressing what they felt. Maybe they were good at it because their feelings were less complicated than mine. Like Kota, I wanted to hug Mamá and smother her with kisses, but at the same time I felt like Avi: so mad I didn't even want to talk to her. But I couldn't do either, so I acted colder than the ocean the night the Titanic sunk.

Mamá looked like she wanted to explain herself to Avi, but instead ran to the bathroom.

Avi bit her lip as Mamá retched and retched for what seemed like hours. "Mami sick," she said.

When Mamá hobbled back to the couch, Avi wouldn't go to her. Our mamá was either too tired or too patient to insist, and went to sleep.

My stomach rumbled because I hadn't had breakfast yet, so I made a sandwich for Avi and me to share. I took the smallest half. Kota would bring me something from school. After Avi and I ate, Mamá woke up. "Why aren't you in school?" Her voice was scratchy, hoarse.

"There was a fire in the teacher's lounge. The school's closed the rest of the week," I replied, flinching as I thought again of Avi at the school, alone in the room under the stairs.

Mamá didn't see the reflection of my mistakes in my eyes because she went back to sleep.

With nothing else to do, and needing to be quiet for Mamá, Avi and I watched cartoons first, and then *Chespirito* all day. Now that Mamá was home, the ghosts of her absence were stronger and louder than when I didn't know what had happened to her. Because what if she felt better in a couple of days? She'd go back to her two jobs. And then how would I know she wouldn't get sick again and end up at the hospital? I couldn't let her leave my side. Not for a second.

In the afternoon—Mamá had finally slept for a longer spell without throwing up—when I was debating whether to take Avi with me as I picked up Kota from school, someone knocked on the door.

It was Maverick.

"What are you doing here?" I asked, instead of saying what I really felt, which was *Thanks for still being my friend. Thanks for being with me yesterday.*

Maverick got me better than I expected though. "Don't be rude, you silly sevie. I'm with the guys—Blessings and Canyon." He pointed somewhere out in Mr. Chang's garden where his Lost Boys were waiting for him. "We'll walk Kota home from school. Oh! I also brought you this."

He handed me a plate of cookies and a container with food that was still warm. "I thought you would love these milanesas. My parents went to an Argentine restaurant today and brought them back."

I didn't know what to say. The sandwich I had for lunch was still bouncing around my otherwise empty stomach, but I was too proud to accept this food he brought.

Take it for Mamá, I thought, because I couldn't afford to be so prideful right now. With Mamá sick, we'd need all the help we could take.

"Is your mom okay?" he asked. He looked at me in a way that made me want to curl in his arms and cry and cry.

"My mom's very sick," I said.

What was it about Maverick that made me want to tell him all my secrets? Maybe the fact that he didn't judge? Of all the people at school and in the street, he was the only one who saw me, a clueless sevie, and knew I needed help. He didn't just say, *Let me know what you need.* In his simple boy way, he gave the help he could. He was my friend. That was more than enough.

"Do you want me to take Avi out for a bit?"

The sun was gloriously sweet and soft, like melted

gold dripping from the trees and painting the world for the fall. I wanted to be able to drink up that sunshine and gather strength. I had to stay home with Mamá, but Avi didn't have to be cooped up, a captive in a dungeon.

"Okay," I said. "No scooter, though! And bring them back as quickly as possible. Mamá will worry if she wakes up and doesn't see them."

"And you? You can't come out for a few minutes? Does your mom need you to stay with her the whole time?"

I looked over my shoulder to where Mamá slept on the couch. She'd been throwing up all day, and if I left, who knew what might happen to her?

"For now, at least," I said.

"Okay," Maverick replied, "But on Saturday I'll pick you up to jump some tricks on the skateboard."

Maverick interpreted my thin-lipped smile as an excuse, but I couldn't commit to something I might not be able to make.

He and Avi left, and I watched them go, no shadow behind them, like the sun was inside them and they lit up the world as they walked. Those two were special.

"He's such a good friend," Mamá said from the couch.

She looked at me with teary eyes that made me want to have a magic wand. I'd wave it in the air, mutter a few special words, and heal her.

The grownup part of my soul whispered, *But you know there's no magic, right? Look at her! If the doctors sent her home like this, no one else can help her.*

I wanted to punch that voice in the face.

Magic was everywhere. Yes, even in our basement apartment. Kota and Avi believed in it. Mamá believed in it.

Maybe just a little bit of magic existed in this house.

I wish life was simple like in *Peter Pan*, that I could bring a mother home and make everything better. Even Hook wanted one in the book (they always left this out of the play). But a *mother* was here, and she needed help. Who could save her?

Mamá, of course unaware of the thoughts raging in my mind, waved me over to her and patted the couch for me to sit next to her.

"Tell me about your friend," she said in that scratchy voice.

"He's such a fool! So spoiled, Mamá! Can you believe he's the seventh child, the only boy?" I exclaimed, to get rid of the tunnel image in my head. "He doesn't want to grow up! He's like what Peter Pan would've become if Peter had family who loved him."

She laughed, maybe wondering what it must have been like to be so loved and treasured. And then she surprised me. "I'm the youngest of five. The only girl."

I held my breath, waiting for more. She'd never talked about her family. I knew her father died when she was too little to remember him, but I didn't know about anyone else.

"They all loved me so much and I was a fool not to see. I wonder where they are now. What they think of me."

My own confession was on the tip of my tongue. Should I tell her I'd sent a message to her mom?

Just when I was about to spill the words like an offering of healing, she said, "My mom would be so disappointed in me if she saw me like this. I'm glad she's so, so far away."

I couldn't tell her. She would get upset at me for breaking the rules, and honestly, I didn't know if my grandma Fátima had received the message. For all I knew, it was still bouncing around on the internet. Even if she'd received it, she might not want anything to do with us, a bunch of lost girls, the four of us needing so much, all the time.

"Do you miss her? Your mom?" I asked her.

She closed her eyes and pressed her lips together. I knew that gesture. That's what I did every time the sorrow was too much.

Closed eyes, closed way to the soul. The tears couldn't escape. Clamped mouth, no way for the words to leak out and ask for help or accept the hurt.

The powerful mother who could make a police officer nervous with her quiet authority had vanished. Instead, a girl (a big girl, but still) was hurting and needed her mom. But that mom was gone forever. I couldn't do anything to help. Not even a magic cupcake or a golden coin could ease this pain.

☀️·☀️·☀️

When Maverick came back with my sisters, the three of them were smiling like they had been soaring all over Neverland, but like Peter and the Lost Boys, once they returned from their adventures, they acted surprised so much time had gone by.

"The girls already ate," he said. "McKenna drove me to the elementary—don't look at me like that!

We have those built-in booster seats in our van. Then she drove us home to say hi to our mom. She misses having babies."

My sisters came in, carrying toys. A couple of Barbie heads poked out of the armful Avi clutched against her heart.

"My mom gave them those. I hope it's okay."

Kota batted her lashes at Maverick shamelessly. "You're awesome, Mav!" She kissed him on the hand before running to the room. My sisters both wore shiny and colorful princess dresses I'd never seen before.

It wasn't my job to provide food, toys, or dress-up clothes for my sisters, but I felt ashamed that someone ended up giving them what my mom never could although she worked so much.

"You shouldn't spoil them so much," I said as Maverick and I went outside to the stoop to talk. "They're going to think everything's easy. It's not even Christmas yet."

Maverick scowled at me. "Okay, Grandma."

Grandmas were nice. What did he mean I sounded like one?

"Just because you're . . . spoiled . . ." He was beyond spoiled, but I couldn't find a better word. "Doesn't mean everyone else goes about their lives like everything belongs to them. My mom gave us rules for a reason. It's not that I'm not grateful for the toys."

He put a hand in the air to stop my rant. "Whoa, whoa, whoa. Time out!" He made the time-out sign and all. The dork.

Now that I was properly quiet, he continued, "Don't get offended. I said the first word that popped into my mouth because I've been thinking about your grandma all the way here."

"Your grandma?" I said. I was just repeating his words to make sense of what he was saying, but I saw no heads or tails to his rambling.

"My grandma? No! My grandma's in Hawaii!" He pointed straight into my chest, and self-consciously I crossed my arms. "*Your* grandma! I got this in my email just now."

He handed me an envelope with my name scribbled on it in what could only be Maverick's handwriting. No grandma ever used such horrible chicken scratches.

"My grandma sent you this?" Okay, miracles could happen, but this was just too much. No way he had received this envelope in his email. What did he think I was?

Maverick burst out laughing. He snatched the envelope back and pulled out a sheet of printed-out paper. "This! I got a message from your grandma and printed it out so you could read it. Get it?"

I clenched my teeth so that when I spoke, my words sounded like hail. "Thanks for laughing at me." I could feel steam seething out of my ears.

"You're missing the whole point! Read it!" He was acting way too excited.

"Did you read it?"

Of course he had. Still, he had the decency to look embarrassed. "Even if I didn't want to, it was a little hard not to. It's good news. Go ahead, read it."

I peeked inside. Mamá still slept. I hoped she hadn't heard this conversation. But she'd been asleep for a while after taking her medicine. The girls were quietly playing in the room, behaving super well— scared I'd take the toys away, I assumed. But why spoil their fun just because I couldn't have any? Just because my needs wouldn't be fixed with a Barbie doll?

I gazed down at the letter. It wasn't very long, but it took me a while to read because it was in Spanish, and some words were hard to understand.

My dearest Minerva,

I can't tell you the surprise I felt when I heard from you. I'm so worried about you and your sisters. Most of all, I'm worried about my dear Natalia. I'm afraid something terrible must have happened to her to leave you unattended. My daughter and I haven't always seen eye to eye concerning many issues, but she's a wonderful mother. A much better mother than I've ever been.

I've been calling the number you provided, but I can't get through. Can you call me instead?

I'll be anxiously waiting by the phone.

Abuela Fátima

The words swam on the page. I willed them to go back to where they belonged. To fulfill their one job. I took a few deep breaths, and then I looked up at Maverick.

"She says my number doesn't work. I'll go check."

Before he could interrupt me, I sneaked back inside. Mamá wasn't on the couch anymore. The bathroom light was on, leaking under the door, but for now, no sounds of sickness echoed. The girls still played quietly in our room.

I grabbed the phone receiver and put it against my ear. It was dead. No tone. Not even the swooshing sound of the ocean.

I tiptoed out of the house to where Maverick waited, sitting on the stairs with his head in his hands.

"It doesn't work," I said. I wasn't sure why I was gasping for air.

He looked up at me with his hands pressing on his cheeks, like a real-life emoji. "I could have told you that if you'd given me the chance. I only called you three hundred times on my way here."

It took all of my concentration to understand what he was saying because my mind was still inside with the dead phone. Maybe it was disconnected because we hadn't paid.

The fifty dollars I'd used for the play were a stone around my neck, sinking me lower in the mud of desperation. I'd have to get it back as soon as possible. Fifty dollars could get us groceries for a week if I was super creative by clipping coupons and buying the cheapest stuff I could get. What had I been thinking spending them on the play?

"Literally, Miranda," Maverick said in a perfect Mr. Beck impersonation. "You're not your bright, perky self. Here. Use my phone." He handed me his cell phone. Of course it was a shiny thing with no buttons. I'd never touched anything so expensive in my life. Well, maybe the arcade game, but that had been at his house too.

The numbers and dollar signs popped in my mind.

"Do you even know what you're saying? That call would cost you a fortune!"

He was shaking his head before I had time to finish my thoughts. "There's an app that lets me call long distance over Wi-Fi. You're seriously technologically deprived."

Of course he'd noticed. I might as well tell him the whole truth. "We don't have Wi-Fi in case you were wondering."

"Your neighbor does, and he let me have the password."

Mr. Chang, our elderly neighbor, threw parties until three in the morning and had Wi-Fi. Of course.

"Let's call her now," he said.

He dialed and handed me back this thing he called a phone. The phone made a different ringing sound from what I was used to. I imagined the sound waves crossing thousands of miles to a satellite in space and then back to planet Earth. Thousands of miles away from me, my grandmother would answer the phone.

And then . . . What would I say?

If it wasn't because I didn't want to ruin Maverick's phone, I would have dropped it. But right at that moment, a voice answered, so similar to my mom's that I looked behind me to make sure she hadn't left the couch. "Hola? Minerva? Sos vos?"

Her voice had a lilt that sometimes Mamá got if she hung out with other Argentines for a while. I loved it. It was like a little song that made me think of warm weather and parties, like the one Mr. Chang had last night.

"Minerva?" the lady asked when I didn't reply.

Maverick made stupid gestures for me to speak.

I didn't know what to call her. *Fátima* seemed too intimate. *Abuela* was more than a foreign word. It was what my friends called their twice-over-moms, and I never had one, had never even had an aunt.

"Soy yo," I said, trying to make my words extra clear to understand.

"Is your mom still missing?" she asked.

I shook my head, and then realized she couldn't see me.

Maverick gave me some privacy and went upstairs to the sidewalk.

"She's home, but she's very sick," I said with the sound of Maverick jumping off and landing on his skateboard in the background. Each time he landed on the pavement of the driveway, there was a SMACK! SMACK!

I looked over my shoulder, afraid my mom would overhear and think I was betraying her. She tried so hard to make it work, but she couldn't do it alone. Now, if my dad had stayed around, or if Mamá had remarried, we wouldn't be in this situation, but every time I asked her why she didn't date, Mamá's eyes flashed and she said she couldn't trust anyone, that she'd never bring a stranger to our house.

"Minerva? What's wrong with her?" the lady, my grandmother, asked. "Is she in the hospital?"

I cleared my throat and covered the phone with my cupped hand. I didn't want Mamá to overhear. "She was in the hospital but came home yesterday. She can't even eat. I'm afraid she'll have to go back."

Although I didn't see the lady who was my grandma, I felt her thinking about what to do. But what could she do? She lived at the other end of the world.

"Let me arrange a few things. Can you send me your address over the email?"

I had no idea why she needed our address. Maybe to send someone to help us. A part of me breathed easier.

I had asked for help and I had received a promise, or at least, the hint of a promise. Someone else shared this burden.

Why did I feel like I was betraying my mom when she needed my loyalty the most?

Chapter 16

Leading the Lost Girls— Enter the Amazons

On Saturday, Maverick stopped by the house to see if I wanted to hang out.

"I can't go," I said.

"Why not? The guys and I are planning a great day. We'll jump on the skateboard and I'll teach you how. I promise it'll be wonderful." Maverick, channeling his inner Kota, stomped on the ground for emphasis.

Before I could stop her spilling our secrets, Kota snuck out from behind me and said, "She can't go because Mamá passed out in the bathroom last night and Minnie had to pretty much drag her to the bed. She's been sleeping ever since."

Maverick's face fell. "Should we call 9-1-1?"

9-1-1. I had almost dialed the number a million

times only to hang up. Even without a working dial tone, the phone could still call emergency services. But then what?

Maverick's mom would let us stay at her house. But after a couple of days, what would we do? Three girls are a lot of people.

Also, Mamá had made me promise not to call the ambulance. We couldn't afford it.

"No," I said. "But check your email. My grandma said to call her today. She must've written something."

I could say that phrase "my grandma" in English, no problem. But I couldn't call her *Abuela* when I talked to her or even thought about her.

"Why are you talking about Grandma Fati?" Kota asked.

"Shoo!" I waved her back into the house, but since I was laughing, my voice didn't have that edge it needed for my sister to obey. Grandma Fati? This girl killed me.

"Maverick, would you do me a huge favor? Do you know where the new girl, the girl from Mexico lives?" I needed to get Mamá's money back.

"Jasmine?" Maverick asked, blushing like a poppy.

He liked girls. I got it. He liked them all, pretty like Bailey and this Jasmine girl. But he was my friend, right? So I pushed this ugly worm of jealousy down into my heart where it went to silently gnaw the darkness inside me.

"What do you need her for?" he asked.

"I just need to ask her something."

He eyed me with suspicion. "Okay, but I don't understand why you want her. In any case, here, I'll leave my skateboard so you can practice."

He placed the skateboard against the doorframe and ran upstairs, out of sight.

☀ ☀ ☀

The girls played until they were too tired to even protest when I told them they needed a bath. In the bathtub, Avi chattered like a squirrel. I ran between the bathroom and the kitchen, checking on the girls and Mamá. By the way my sisters laughed when they saw me, I guessed I must have looked like a chicken with its head cut off. (Okay, I'd never seen one, but Mamá had terrible stories about her next-door neighbor chopping off chicken heads.)

The girls splashed all over the bathroom and squealed when I popped my head in to tell them off. On the couch, Mamá gazed into space with a sad smile on her lips, as if Avi's words were heavenly music.

I was used to the miracle of her voice already, so it didn't surprise me anymore. When had that happened? Miracles were all around me that I hadn't seen before, and I wasn't even talking about magic cupcakes or golden coins under the pillow. We still had a roof over our heads, and Mamá was home. We had eaten today.

"She doesn't forgive me," Mamá whispered, startling me out of my blessings count. "I don't blame her. I hardly forgive myself."

Her tears fell heavily on the pillow, making a little puddle before the fabric sucked them in. I wished the cotton/poly blend also could take away Mamá's sorrow. Maybe if she weren't so sad, she'd heal sooner.

"Tell me what you and the girls did while I was gone," Mamá asked.

I'd already told her some things. Not the part where I took Avi to school and then there was a fire, but I spared no details when I told her how I stopped taking Avi to Mirta's.

"She owed me money and said she'd watch Avi. That's why I still took her there," Mamá said. I felt she was confessing to me, justifying her actions.

That free care turned out to be too expensive for baby Avi to pay, but how could I add to Mamá's sorrow?

Later, when the girls were in bed, Mamá felt a little better. Enough to sit up on the couch. "Let me braid your hair," she said. And after a few seconds' silence, she added, "I'm sorry I didn't braid your hair for the audition that day. I'm so sorry."

I couldn't see her face, but her hands trembled against the skin of my neck.

"So did you try out? What part did you get?" she asked.

"I'm not going to be in the play," I said.

She took me by the shoulders and turned me around so she could look me in the eyes. "But why? You talked about this play for weeks. Why aren't you going to participate?"

I bit my lip as I debated whether to tell her or not. I couldn't participate because she was sick. I couldn't leave her alone.

What about school? the nasty voice spoke in my mind again. I shooed it away, but it stayed, lurking in a corner of my heart.

Maybe Mamá didn't need me to say anything to understand what I was thinking. She was my mom. She knew me better than anyone.

And then she said something that surprised me. "I hope there's never a next time, but if I get sick, ask for help. You're so young, Minerva," she said. "I'm sorry you had to grow up so quickly."

I was twelve, and although my body was just now starting to change into something else, I was still powerless to take care of my family.

Later, Mamá slept, but I kept watch into the night. I went over the *Peter Pan and Wendy* book. Some parts I hated (like the dialogs where I didn't know who was saying what), but I kept going back to Tiger Lily. Did she really only say *How* in the book? What was her story, really?

The book said that Peter found her tied to a rock in the middle of the sea. Captain Hook had left her there after she tried to raid the boat with her horde of Indians. Horde of Indians? So offensive! If this book was written today, this kind of disrespect wouldn't pass, I hoped.

It would be a million times better if Mrs. Santos went along with my idea: instead of Indians, Tiger Lily (we'd just call her Lily) would lead a band of sisters, smashing down gender roles and fighting the stupid Lost Boys.

That way Tiger Lily wouldn't have to call Peter

the *Great White Father*. This story was awesome, but it was phrases like this that made me want to cry. Or laugh. I actually snorted and máte tea flew out of my nose. But she was strong, that Tiger Lily. She took care of her people. I knew what she felt. She just needed a makeover for the twenty-first century.

☀·☀·☀

The weekend was eternal—even longer than when Mamá was gone. Waiting for a message and hearing nothing in return turns time into syrup.

Sticky.

Slow.

Thick.

At night, I couldn't sleep. I read the stupid *Peter and Wendy* book so many times I memorized the whole thing.

Each time I read it, I realized that Wendy wasn't the part for me after all. Who wanted a band of Lost Boys when I already mothered a band of lost girls, including Mamá? She was fading away.

Becoming Peter's romantic interest or the reason he gave up his eternal childhood didn't interest me either. I wanted to be free. I wanted to keep fighting

Captain Hook and his pirates. Like Tiger Lily surely did, once Peter gave up Neverland.

That Lily girl wasn't only beautiful; she was also smart. Otherwise, how would she have been made the chieftain of her people? She was the daughter of Great Little Panther, after all.

Even if I couldn't bring Lily to life in the play, I'd fight like her, until the end. I'd find a way to stop the hook of illness and loneliness from hurting my mom once and for all.

Chapter 17

Not Even Magic Can Fix This

ON SUNDAY AFTERNOON, Mamá felt good enough to walk a little. She sat on a rickety chair in Mr. Chang's yard and looked on as Avi and Kota built fairy houses. The weather forecast announced a cold front coming soon. The mountains were already dressed in their white capes, and when the wind blew down on the valley, it carried a warning to snuggle close to someone, to put on warm winter clothes.

Wordlessly, Avi had brought Mamá the blanket Mrs. Sorensen had given her. Mamá wrapped herself in it, like they were the words Avi withheld from her.

I wondered why Avi wouldn't talk to Mamá. Why she wouldn't even whisper a word in her presence.

Mamá must have wondered, too. She gazed at

the fluffy, cottony clouds with such longing, as if she wanted to fly away. I had a feeling she would if it weren't for us tying her down to earth. Her skin was so pale. Even her hair had started to bleach out of color. In the sunshine, I noticed some grays that hadn't been there before she got sick.

When the mountains were orange and gold with the last fingertips of sunshine, Mamá walked back inside the house.

"You can play outside a few more minutes. It's too cold for me," she said.

Avi and Kota jumped on fall leaves with their bare feet, as if they didn't notice the bite of cold. Neither did I, for that matter, but my burst of warmth came at the sight of Maverick and Jasmine, walking in my direction, and Jasmine's brother, Miguel, trailing behind.

Maverick didn't speak Spanish, and Jasmine's English still had a way to go before she could provoke such a fit of laughter, but Maverick was cracking up like she had told him *THE* joke of the century.

When he was just a few yards away, he pointed and said, "Here's Jasmine. I told her you wanted to talk with her."

"Mavvy come play!" Avi called him over, and he

took off running to help them build what had now turned into Fairytown. Miguel followed him like a shadow.

Jasmine swiped her hair out of her face. It fell like a shiny waterfall behind her back. It was so black, blue streaks gleamed in it.

"Hola," I said, suddenly nervous. My Spanish wasn't the best, at least not like Jasmine's, but I'd give it a try. "¿Cómo estás?"

She made a gesture of approval with her head, nodding up and down, and then winking at me. "I like your accent," she said in Spanish. "My mom likes to watch the Argentine telenovelas."

"Mine loves the Mexican ones," I said. "And my sisters and I love *Chespirito*."

"Chido!" she said, and the little awkwardness that had separated us a second ago was gone.

Who knew telenovelas were the unifying force for Spanish-speaking countries?

She looked at me expectantly. Somehow, Maverick must have told her something about why I wanted to meet her. I didn't know how to start, but she said, "So, ¿qué onda?"

Self-conscious of my Argentine accent, I continued speaking Spanish. "Do you want to be in the middle school play? If you want to fit in at school, being in the play is the easiest, fastest way."

Jasmine's face froze in shock. "The play?"

Something had definitely been lost in translation. It was clear she hadn't been expecting an offer to be in the play, the event of the season. She crossed her arms in front of her like she needed a shield, like she was scared of me, although we were the same height.

"Hear me out," I said, placing a hand on her arm. It always worked when I needed to calm down one of my sisters. "I got cast as Tiger Lily, but I can't do it anymore. It's a cool role, though. If you want it, you can have my part. There's a fifty-dollar fee. I made a commitment, but Miss Santos said I had to find a replacement." I added the last part quickly because I saw that she was about to argue.

Jasmine wasn't convinced. "I don't know . . ." Her narrowed eyes watched me carefully, as if she were trying to discover a trick, a trap. "If she's so cool, why don't you want to be her anymore?"

She had a point.

I wasn't about to tell her my personal problems, but she deserved a true answer, even if it wasn't the whole thing. "I can't go to rehearsals. I have to babysit because my mom's sick."

Her face softened in understanding, but then her eyes sharpened again, as if she'd remembered something. "But Tiger Lily? I don't love the Disney movie."

Bingo! Jasmine was the perfect girl for the role, then.

I explained my idea: of a band of Amazons that beat the Lost Boys, pirates, and mermaids at everything.

Jasmine thought for a second.

"I'll help you get ready. I promise," I said. "I'm envisioning Wonder Woman-like outfits for all the Amazons." I added that last part in the spur of the moment.

Jasmine closed her eyes for a few seconds, as if trying to picture herself on a stage, in a new school, in a language she still didn't entirely speak. She let out a long sigh, and I held my breath.

Finally, she stretched out her hand for me to shake. "Deal. I'll bring the money to school tomorrow. Is that okay?"

"Okay," I said. The burden of Lily and her girls fell off my shoulders.

A true warrior knows when to step aside. I was already fighting too many battles. Jasmine seemed like a fighter, too. She'd be the perfect Tiger Lily.

So while Maverick and Miguel helped the girls make piles of leaves for the fairies to hide, I told Jasmine all the amazing things about Tiger Lily. And all the changes Jasmine could make to her character.

With each word out of my mouth, my heart crumbled to smaller pieces. By the time I was done telling Jasmine about Lily's awesomeness, my new friend was smiling from ear to ear.

Lily wasn't an idiot. She was brave. Her girls counted on her, and she protected them.

I'd read the book so many times, and I'd still been so clueless.

Lily, if one could read beyond the author's intentions, was the coolest person in the whole Neverland universe.

❋⋅❋⋅❋

The next day Mamá must have felt tons better because her usual bossy, no-nonsense self had been busily occupied cleaning the house by the time I woke up.

"Mamá, go back to bed," I said.

She clicked her tongue and shook her head. "You can't miss so much school. I won't allow it."

"But, Avi," I argued, trying to take the broom out

of her hand while my baby sister clutched my other hand like I was her savior and my mom a cannibal ready to eat her or something.

"I'm the mom! I know what to do. Go to school and don't come back until three. Remember, that cop will be more than happy to catch you as a truant."

She was the mom. I was the daughter.

I couldn't argue with that, so I left with Maverick and Kota, while Avi wailed inside the house, not in words—that would have made her yelling and crying more bearable for Mamá, I think—but in shrieks and howls that rang in my ears for the whole morning.

On the way to English, right after lunch, Mrs. Burke, the vice principal, saw me in the hallway. I'd never spoken to her, even though she welcomed the students at the school doors every morning. I'd always tried to blend in so I wouldn't call attention to myself. But she obviously knew me.

She wagged a finger at me like she was accusing me of something bad. Really bad. Her face was so serious. Her light brown eyes x-rayed me, and I started sweating all over.

She didn't need to call me. I walked in her direction, and she tucked her highlighted hair behind an ear in which dangled a single elegant pearl pendant.

"So you're the famous Minerva Miranda," she said.

I nodded. My tongue was glued to the roof of my mouth.

"Mrs. Santos has told me all about you."

I had a hard time swallowing.

She continued, "She shared those Internet articles with me. We love your idea of having Amazons instead of Indians. For months since I started this job, I've been thinking about how to get the school to change this play tradition. And you figured something out. Thank you."

I was giddy with the compliment, and by now my heart rate had gone back to normal, and my tongue was unstuck. Pride, confidence, and an unstuck tongue weren't always a good combination. Proof of that was the reply that blurted out of me before I could think better of it.

"My mom says sometimes people do things out of habit," I said. "Even when they affect us, we go with the flow because ignoring things is easier than working to fix them. I didn't want to go with the flow."

In my mind, I could hear Kota exclaiming, *Minerva Soledad! A single thank you would have been enough!*

To my surprise, Mrs. Burke nodded. "It's time

for change, and I thank you for fighting for it. I've always hated *Peter Pan*, but now, if the play turns out as cool as it reads from the new draft Mrs. Santos wrote, I might bring my family to come watch it."

Her words filled me with pride. Now I was committed to making this new Lily into the star of the play.

"I wish you'd agreed to stay on as Tiger Lily—" she said.

"Just Lily," I said. If we were going to implement all these changes, we might as well start by calling our characters their proper names.

Mrs. Burke smiled slyly. "Okay, Lily. While I'm not happy you're not in the play, I can't say you found a bad replacement. Jasmine Garcia is a great addition."

"Jasmine was the clear next option," I said, shrugging my shoulder. "The role had to go to a strong girl, and Jasmine is the strongest girl I know."

Mrs. Burke squinted at me like she was seeing me for the first time, and maybe she was. I hated that she might find me lacking. "I know another pretty strong young lady, who's talking to me right now."

I held her gaze. Without a mask to hide me, the true Minerva, I said, "Sometimes a girl gets tired of being strong all the time and just wants to be a kid, you know?"

She smiled warmly and ruffled my hair. "Now we're talking, sister," she said, then turned on her kitten heels and walked away.

☀·☀·☀

By lunchtime, I realized my replacement lacked the fury required to face off Captain James Hook and his pirates. In spite of her swagger the day we transferred Lilyhood, in front of the whole cast, Jasmine was too shy. Too soft.

"You have to think that she wanted to achieve two things," I said. We were in the drama closet going through props. "First, she hates those pirates that came to her land to pillage and take away her girls' pride. Second, she maybe wants food. Think about it, her land is rich beyond thought. But the pirates are stealing from the Amazons. She wants to prove you can't mess with her people and expect to tell the tale."

Jasmine nodded, but I didn't have the impression that I was getting through to her. Miguel, on the other hand, was drinking up my words. In silence, he organized a box with props for the play. Flowers. Plastic swords. Hats. Eye patches.

"Too bad this is all old stuff," Maverick said. "We could have done with a new cannon or something."

"¿Estás loco?" Miguel exclaimed, brandishing a sword. "We have plenty and more. But this? This goes in the trash."

Miguel held up the Indian headdress that countless Tiger Lilys had worn for generations and generations of Andromeda Middle School productions. Miguel pushed the colorful feathers deep in the trashcan. "We'll make Lily and her warriors true warriors, wonder women all of them. You'll see," he said in Spanish, and I translated to Maverick.

There was a glint in Miguel's eye that told me he got it. The props and costumes were safe in his hands.

My mom always said that necessity was the mother of invention, and Miguel was proof of that. He was a year older than Jasmine, but for some reason, they were both in my grade. Miguel had that older sibling attitude I knew too well.

Looking at the headdress with disdain, Jasmine said, "And you got all of that about Lily from the one line that says she was captured while trying to raid the boat and when she says 'How'?"

"It's called subtext," I said, distracted by the movement beside me.

Miguel put down a flashlight and an old bell he'd found in the bottom of the box. He exclaimed wordlessly, making expressive gestures that left no room for doubting that he was excited to have found the props for Tinker Bell.

An idea struck immediately, and I acted upon it. "Miguel," I said, "since you're good at actions, why don't you teach Jasmine some fierce facial expressions? Think about pirates trying to take your land. Your customs and religion. Make it clear that she's having none of that."

A somber look passed over Jasmine. "What about having to leave them? Your land and your people. Your dog named Coco and your next-door neighbor Gabriel, who's been your best friend forever? What if you had to walk the desert, hiding from searching lights? Being afraid that they'll take you away from your family at the border. Do those feelings count?"

Fierceness shone in her deep brown eyes. I didn't look away. I couldn't. I knew what she felt, even though our situations were so different. Jasmine, the soft. Jasmine the sweet. She was strong in ways I couldn't imagine.

"Those feelings are perfect. Channel that," I said, patting her shoulder, and left them practicing facial expressions. By rehearsal tonight, she would have perfected Lily.

Before the bell for the end of lunch, I called home to check on Mamá and Avi. The line was working again.

"We're good. We're good," Mamá replied, her attempt at cheerfulness not fooling me.

Avi still wailed in the background. How in the world were her vocal chords still working? Poor Avi. She missed me. Poor Mamá. Stuck all day with a baby who hated her.

"I'm starting to think a visit to Mirta might do both of us good." Mamá laughed, but I didn't join her.

She knew what my silence meant because she added, "It's a joke, Minnie. It's a joke. I won't take her back but—Santo Cielo!—I sure need a break."

So that evening, instead of hanging out with Jasmine, Miguel, Maverick, and Blessings, I stayed home to give Mamá what she needed. A break.

Avi didn't even want to look at Mamá. In fact, every time Mamá looked her way, Avi broke into hysterics.

"Can you take her outside for a minute? Maybe

she needs some sunshine," Mamá whispered. She was back on the couch. My productive, busy mom hadn't made it all the way to the afternoon.

"Avi, put on your coat!"

The little dictator smiled and didn't wait to be told twice. Once outside, she ran to Fairytown and pointed. "Look, Minnie. Fairy house!"

Someone had made a little wall with river rocks to fence off the area around the houses. A beautiful rosebush heavy with velvety red flowers covered the fairy house like a canopy. The flowers were so out of season I looked around to make sure we'd walked out in the right place and time. But the mountains were still covered in snow, and the chill bit the end of my nose. Roses in October? I'd never noticed this bush before.

"Did the fairies make this?" I asked, surprise leaking into my voice.

Avi laughed and pointed to Mr. Chang, working in his apple trees. "He built it, Minnie! Fairies too small, Minnie!"

I laughed. She was right. Even though they were magical, fairies were too small to do some things.

I waved at Mr. Chang, hoping he knew how much I appreciated his quiet presence. I'd never thanked him for the vegetables. He waved back, and his smile said he knew I was grateful.

Avi played in the leaves and jumped in puddles. She spoke with her imaginary friends. I eyed the skateboard Maverick had left by the door, but every time I wanted to try it, to at least step on it, I imagined someone casually walking past my house and seeing a ridiculous twelve-year-old girl trying to learn how to ride a skateboard.

But it was now or never. Maverick would surely miss his skateboard soon. He'd come back for it and then I wouldn't get to try it at all. I'd be too proud to borrow it again.

Avi was stacking petals on a flat rock, so I made my way to the skateboard. As soon as I grabbed it, the door opened with a crash and Kota yelled, "Call 9-1-1! Mamá is dead!"

☀·☀·☀

Mr. Chang called 9-1-1.

Mr. Chang held Avi, who was paralyzed with horror and all the regret a three-year-old could hold. "Mamá. Mamá," she mumbled.

But Mamá didn't respond.

Mr. Chang ran into our apartment and said into his phone, "She's alive, officer. But hurry up!"

Mamá looked like Snow White after biting the poisoned apple. Mr. Chang gathered us around him and called the neighbors to help. A lady from across the street stayed with Mamá.

My sisters and I waited in Mr. Chang's kitchen while he spoke softly on the phone. I was so sick with worry that after everything was over, Kota and I said later how weird it was that we'd been inside Mr. Chang's kitchen but couldn't remember what it looked like.

Soon after the ambulance parted with its tragic wail and our sleeping mother, Maverick's mom showed up with open arms where Avi found refuge. McKenna held Kota and they both cried quietly next to the window.

"Let's get a backpack with your things, girls," Mrs. Sorensen said.

I looked at her and she nodded. Maverick gave me the thumbs up. "I get to have younger sisters for a few days," he said.

I only thought of Mamá, alone in the hospital.

My sisters and I packed. As we headed to the Sorensens' car, a taxi stopped in front of Mr. Chang's driveway, blocking our exit. I'd never seen a taxi in our neighborhood before.

A lady got out of the car carrying a small suitcase and a big teddy bear. The bear looked ancient, like it belonged to another century. When the lady saw me, transfixed, she pressed her lips hard, just like Mamá did to control her emotions, just like I did to control mine.

"Are you Nati's girls?" she asked in English.

I nodded, taking a step in her direction.

Her lips broke into a grandmotherly smile I recognized because I'd seen it in my dreams. It was the same smile as in her social media profile picture.

"My Minerva!" she cried and ran to wrap me in her arms in a hug that felt like home. "Mi niña! Mi bebé!"

I didn't know this woman. I'd never seen her before, but she smelled of safety. She was our twice-over mother.

"Minnie," Avi said in her small voice.

Behind me, my sisters crowded around Mrs. Sorensen.

"Is she family?" Mrs. Sorensen asked in a polite but oh-so-motherly voice.

I translated back and forth between Mrs. Sorensen

and Abuela Fátima. Abuela opened her purse to reveal her passport and Mamá's birth certificate and most importantly, pictures to prove she was our grandma.

"Here, Natalia's eighteen years old in this picture. This is when she left home. She looks just as beautiful as Minerva, but with sharper eyes, and more developed, of course. Minerva's only twelve," said Abuela Fátima.

As I translated back and forth, I edited to save me embarrassment.

Maverick whispered in my ear, "She said something about beautiful and your name and you left that out. Why is that?"

I elbowed him playfully and he smiled.

"You're welcome to come to my house with the girls and refresh yourself after such a long trip," Mrs. Sorensen offered.

Abuela's eyes glinted. "Thank you, kind lady. But my little girl needs me, you see. I need to get to my Natalia."

When I translated Abuela's words, I thought that when she said *my little girl*, she meant me. It wasn't until the words were out of my mouth that I realized she was talking about my mom, *her* little girl. Like the Lost Boys, my sisters, Mamá, and I needed a mother. A mother for all of us, to help us until we were strong enough to fly solo, without any magic powder.

Chapter 18

Miracles

As soon as I heard Abuela was going to the hospital, I clutched her hand and didn't let go.

"I'll come translate for you," I said, happy to have found an excuse to see my mom.

But I wasn't needed for translation. Abuela made do with the few words she knew in English. I'd never seen a more determined person. After tons of back and forth in English and Spanish, with some universal sign language thrown in and a lot of smiles and thank-yous in between, we navigated the labyrinth of the hospital and reached Mamá's room.

Before I went in, I warned her. "Abuela," I said, savoring the word. It felt too sweet on my tongue. "Mamá doesn't look very well. It might be a shock."

Maybe the words were more for my benefit than Abuela's. The image of Mamá sleeping on the couch, her hand strangely warm in mine, would haunt me forever.

Abuela nodded and squeezed my hand. She wasn't biting her lip anymore. She finally smiled. "We'll support each other, okay?"

Mamá was awake, surprisingly. She looked up at the ceiling, counting something with her fingers.

She must have felt our eyes on her because she turned her gaze to the door. She looked back and forth between Abuela Fátima and me, like she couldn't believe we were there. She finally covered her head with the white sheet before bursting into tears.

"I didn't want you to see me like this!"

I didn't know who she meant, Abuela or me. Maybe both. I swallowed my tears, but Abuela's were running freely down her face.

In two strides Abuela was next to Mamá, holding her hand. "Mi niña! Mi bebé!" She called Mamá the same endearments she'd called me.

I knew why Mamá cried so hard now. When someone who loves you helps carry your burden, you have the luxury of letting go and being vulnerable.

Quietly, I slipped out of the room so they could cry for sorrows carried alone for a long time. I sat in the waiting room for two episodes of *Judge Judy*, and when I went back to the room, I found Abuela and Mamá whispering to each other.

Mamá hugged that tattered teddy bear like she was holding baby Avi. For once in my life, I wasn't jealous that someone else was getting affection and love. If I had felt burdened with responsibility for someone's life for only a few days, what about Mamá, who had no one else to help her out?

※·※·※

Before we headed back home, we stopped briefly at the grocery store. After, we picked up the girls, went home, and in a whirlwind of activity, Abuela Fátima unpacked, cleaned the kitchen, put a load in the washer, and made a tuna salad.

After we ate, Abuela took a shower. When she came out of the bathroom, she looked younger without her smeared makeup and with her reddish-brown hair sticking in all directions.

"You're so pretty, Abuela." I said, setting out the máte tea for her. She'd need some peace and quiet after her trip and visiting the hospital. Although we'd just sat with Mamá, seeing her in pain was emotionally exhausting. I knew *I* needed some kind of pick-me-up after the sadness.

Abuela smiled and beckoned me to her. She opened her purse that hung from the chair, took out a package of chocolate cookies, and offered me the whole thing.

I took only one, but she left the rest next to me. "You're so sweet, Minnie. Is that what the girls call you? You're a good sister. You deserve the first cookies. I didn't have much time to gather stuff to bring, but these were your mom's favorite ones. Your father liked them too."

I processed this information in silence. She knew my father. How many other things did Abuela know? I couldn't wait to ask, but now was not the time.

"I was scared you were someone else pretending to be you, and you'd come here to kidnap us or something."

Abuela nodded. "Yes, I was scared, too. Of not making it in time. But I'm here now. Things will change."

I chewed on the crumbly cookie. It wasn't as sweet as I expected. It was more like dark chocolate. "Kota says sometimes that if you don't ask for help, then no one will help you." I swallowed and then took a sip of the maté she offered. It was sweeter than the one Mamá made. "Mamá says you have to do all you can on your own."

Abuela nodded knowingly. Before replying, she took some knitting from her purse. It was clear where Mamá got her restless hands and feet. Like Mamá, Abuela was always doing something.

"It's good to know how to do things on your own, but many times, you don't have to suffer. You can rely on people, too. No one can do everything on their own. Even *I* had some extra help getting here."

"How, Abuela?"

Abuela drank her máte. "A few months ago, I had a dream about you."

"Me? But you never knew me."

"I'd seen pictures of you. Our souls are wiser than our minds. I believe we visit our loved ones when we dream. In this dream, you were flying like a fairy. You stopped midflight and told me to get my passport. And so I did. For a while I had known your mom lived in this area. I opened the Facebook account to see if I could learn anything about her.

"The last time we talked, I said some horrible things to her. They were the truth, or what I thought was the truth. I won the argument, but I lost my daughter and my precious granddaughters. At the time, it was only you and Dakota. Your father and I never got along, and when he left your mother, she thought I would gloat. A few years later, someone told me of Avalon's birth and said your mom was too embarrassed to reach out for help. I was hurt that she wouldn't. Time made it harder to reach out, and now, here we are."

We continued taking turns drinking máte.

"I had money saved up. Like a miracle, I never lacked for work. For a woman my age to be employed by a government agency, and to be indispensable? That's something unheard of in Argentina. I learned all I could about computers, and then I did my best every day at work. I had money and vacation days saved up, and when I received your message, I didn't hesitate. Without knowing, I'd been getting ready for a long time."

Miracles weren't just magic cupcakes or a shadowless boy, they were having the inspiration to do something and actually doing it.

☀·☀·☀

The next days and weeks were a complete turn of the page for my sisters and me. But soon, we settled into a routine.

Abuela made me go to school every day. After Kota and I were gone, she'd go to the hospital with Avi to see Mamá.

Surprisingly, Avi didn't throw any fits with Abuela, and when told to, she'd even give Mamá a kiss. By the time we came home from school, the apartment smelled delicious. Even better than the Sorensens'. Instead of bringing us food, now it was Maverick who stayed to eat dinner at our house, and I loved it.

But Mamá was still very sick. So sick that the doctors sent her home because they said there was nothing else they could do for her.

Abuela Fátima didn't despair. "We'll get a different opinion. Things will work out."

I didn't see how, but Abuela didn't want to tell me anything when I asked. She and Mamá spoke until late into the night, and when I wanted to eavesdrop, Abuela sent me to sleep.

I'd obey, only to wake up with the sound of Mamá's nightmares. She'd wake up crying like La Llorona. "Where are my nenas?" Her fear scared me silly.

Little by little, Mamá was leaving. But she didn't want to.

No amount of wishing or begging the fairies for a miracle would fix her.

❋ ❋ ❋

One day in November, Abuela Fátima said, "We need more than fairy dust to make her feel good."

She was mending socks with determination, as if with each stitch she was mending our lives, too. She muttered and muttered under her breath.

"What are you saying, Abuela?"

"Sometimes I go over things that happened a long time ago in my mind, and I say the things I should have said then. Even if it's too late now." Abuela sighed and threw a mended sock into the basket. One down, three hundred thousand to go. "I was thinking about when I made your mom go back to Argentina with me. Your grandfather had just died, and I was here in this country alone with five young children, all under eighteen. I missed my mother. How selfish, right?"

Her reasons were completely valid. Why had Mamá been so mad?

"Were you happy with your decision?"

Abuela stretched, like her soul needed strength to continue telling the tale. "My four sons went to college there, for free, but my daughter never forgave me for uprooting her."

She took her wallet out of her pocket and showed me a stack of pictures. Four sons, all sharing one or another of Mamá's features. A handful of kids.

"Your cousins, mi amor." Abuela said. "All boys. Twelve boys, can you believe it? All of my kids have three kids each. I'm so glad Natalia had you girls. All her life, all she wanted was a woman of her own blood. I guess she wanted to create her own friends."

A silence fell on the kitchen. Mamá coughed, and I felt Abuela stiffen beside me, attentive to Mamá's every move and sound.

"She can't go on like this much longer," I said, stating the obvious. "The medicines are too expensive, and she can't work anymore."

Abuela and I had never talked about Mamá's illness. Liver failure. She knew that I knew though, even if she tried to keep the truth away from my sisters and me.

I'd overheard conversations and read the prescriptions for the collection of orange medicine plastic containers covering Mamá's nightstand. It wasn't that hard to fill in the lines for the things no one told me.

If the medicines didn't work, then Mamá would need a transplant. She was so sick.

My ears started ringing as if a storm were bellowing around me. I bit my bottom lip hard to stop the tears.

Abuela held my hand, and whispered, "I'm sorry."

I understood then that she'd been waiting for me to figure it out on my own. We couldn't stay in Utah by ourselves. Mamá needed constant care, and we didn't have any help.

Abuela didn't speak the language. She couldn't work. How would we pay the rent?

"I won't take you away from this country like I did with your mother. She said that I stole the best opportunity of her life. She'd be furious if I did the same thing to you, but sweet Minerva, I see no other way."

Abuela didn't press me. She didn't even wait for an answer. She left the facts bouncing on the kitchen table. As if by magic, I saw our future stretch before us: the three of us alone, in a country that was ours but that was so, so hard to live in. In Argentina, we had a huge family. Mamá could rest. She could heal. They had great schools there. We'd be okay.

But Maverick, and the play at the end of the week, right before the Thanksgiving break. . . . With so much going on, time had gone by fast. My plan of becoming the first Latina president of the United States was now on pause for who knew how long.

I sat by the window, wishing this decision were easy. Outside, a bunch of fireflies danced around the fairy shelter. Fireflies in the fall. I'd never seen one even in the summer! I held my breath as I watched them. I felt a tiny hand on my shoulder, and when I turned, there was Avi, her eyes ablaze by the sight outside, the fairies dancing in the swirling autumn leaves.

"See, Minnie? Fairy so, so nice! She go home with us."

☀ ☀ ☀

A few days later, I told Abuela the news during breakfast. Her spoon clanked on her dish and her hands flew to her mouth. "Seriously, mi amor? You would do that?"

I nodded. "I love this country, but it would be super nice to have a family, a big extended family, too. If Mamá says we should go, of course we'll go."

Abuela came around the table and hugged me. "You're a very mature little girl. I'm proud of you."

After the play tonight, I was ready to go. Until it was time for college, and then the world better watch out. I still had big plans.

"Will you be at the play?" I asked Abuela for like the thousandth time. "At least for the first showing?"

I had prepared for no one from my family coming to see it. Mamá was sick, and Abuela couldn't leave her alone. Besides, I didn't have a part, really. After making sure Jasmine had an idea of what I meant by Amazons, I hadn't been to a single rehearsal. Mrs. Santos let me flash the light and ring the bell that was supposed to be Tinker Bell. It wasn't a big deal, and anyone could take that spot, but it had made me feel part of my group of friends.

Abuela clapped her hands. "We'll be there for all three shows! We wouldn't miss the most important play in the whole world for anything."

I knew she was exaggerating. She would miss it for Mamá. "What about Mamá?"

Mamá surprised me with a hug from behind. I was so used to seeing her not walking around, that I never imagined she'd get up.

"We'll be there," she whispered in my ear.

"But how?"

"Mr. Chang said he'd give us a ride, and I have the wheelchair the hospital lent me. We'll be fine."

Now that Mamá was going to the play, I wished I could show her what a strong, fearsome warrior I'd become. Lily on the stage, blaring to the four winds, protecting my family against the pirates, the Lost Boys, and even the mermaids.

It was too late now.

❄ ❄ ❄

I was at the school way early to make sure Miguel and Maverick had everything ready: the bell, the flashlight, the piece of metal that made a sound like a storm, two bottles filled at different heights to make the sound of the clock when he banged on them with a wooden stick. A fan to fly Lily's hair around and make her look fierce.

The first two shows went smoothly.

Jasmine as Lily was breathtaking. She'd been reading about Tiger Lily (there were books about her!) and Diana from Wonder Woman and the other mythical Amazonians. Not only that, but Jasmine had found out about real-life women warriors like

Pine Leaf, Running Eagle, and Rosana Chouteau. This last one, of the Osage Nation, had said, "I think my band obey me better than they would a man."

Jasmine was ready for her role. One of her lines— *Leave my people alone!*—paralyzed the room.

Good thing we'd been able to change it from the stupid "How."

After every Lily scene, I clapped so hard my hands itched later, and when I saw Jasmine, I hugged her and told her she'd been wonderful. She must not have heard the envy in my voice, but I felt it. Why had I been so silly?

Wendy was wonderful, as expected. I still thought Maverick would have made a better Peter than Blessings, but I couldn't deny that Maverick rocked the lights and the sound effects that were too complicated for Miguel and me to improvise.

Everyone clapped and cheered when Lily yelled, "Get out of my land!"

The hairs on my arms stood like needles and a knot formed in my throat when Jasmine got the only standing ovation in the last bow.

"Maybe next year we can put out a different production. I think our school's ready to evolve beyond

Peter Pan," Mrs. Santos said with a small smile, clapping next to me. "An original adaptation of *Lily*, or an *Alice's Adventures in Wonderland* set in the modern world. Or even better, a gender-bending *Little Prince* . . . . What do you think?"

I clenched my teeth to stifle an exclamation of disappointment. I wouldn't be here to enjoy it.

Mrs. Santos must have understood my expression. "Don't worry," she said. "I intend to keep your contact information handy to consult with you. Your insights into *Peter Pan* were genius."

"If you do *The Little Prince*, cast Maverick as the Fox," I said. "He's the best friend a person could have."

☀ ☀ ☀

The next day, for the last performance, there was bad news.

"Wendy is sick," Jasmine said as soon as she saw me walk into the auditorium.

It took me a minute to understand what she was talking about. Mamá had been sick for so long, I never considered that anyone else could be sick too. "What do you mean? It can't be that bad," I brushed her off.

"You don't understand. Bailey has food poisoning. She'll be okay, but she can't perform tonight."

Mrs. Santos was frantic when she met me. "I need you! You're the only one who can save us!" she exclaimed, holding me by the shoulders.

It was too amazing to be true. Now that I was ready to leave everything behind, now that the whole student council election meant nothing because at this time tomorrow I would be on a plane to summertime, to the other side of the world, *now* I got this chance.

Wendy Darling.

Kota had taught me to accept blessings when they came, and this was my parting gift from whoever it was that listened to girls in need, girls who'd never even gotten a golden coin from the Tooth Fairy.

Poor Bailey Cooper, sick at home. She would have so many other opportunities, though. And I couldn't miss this chance. I'd let Tiger Lily go. I wasn't going to make the same mistake twice.

"Okay, Mrs. Santos," I said. "I'm ready."

☀ ☀ ☀

Sometime around the middle of the play, I forgot to speak with an English accent.

I truly believed I was flying over Neverland, watching my little brothers, admiring the brave Lily. My Wendy wasn't jealous of her at all. It was admiration all around.

I didn't have to pretend to be enchanted by the light of Tinker Bell or her chime-like voice. She was magical, and I was so grateful for Maverick's brilliance in remembering the right cues for the tiny fairy. With the haste of being on stage, I'd forgotten to remind him, but everything turned out perfectly.

At the end, when Wendy and her siblings and all the Lost Boys were safe in London, I gazed at the audience, and improvised. "I believe in fairies! I do! I do!"

The whole audience chanted with me, "I do! I do!" I knew that among the faces I couldn't really see were Mamá and Abuela, clapping like little girls, along with my sisters.

The ovation at the end was as thunderous as it had been during the first two showings. I bowed and curtsied and held Maverick's hand as we weaved through the audience to find my mom.

Mr. Chang had seen the show too, and he had a bouquet of flowers for me. The sweet perfume made me blush. I felt like a señorita. Now that my childhood was almost behind me, a pang of longing settled in my chest. The star inside me glowed softly, making my cheeks warm, telling me everything would be okay.

"You were wonderful!" Mamá said, emotional and glowy-eyed. "You were the perfect Wendy."

Kota shrugged. "You know how to act. That's for sure. Who knew you could be that sweet after all?"

Like a clown, I stuck out my tongue at Kota. We both laughed.

"The real star was Maverick," I said. "He even remembered about the fairy."

Maverick's face turned bright red. "What do you mean? That was Miguel."

Miguel was just crossing ahead of us. "Miguel! Come here!" I called.

He bounded in our direction, followed by a trail of little boys who looked exactly like him. Apparently, Jasmine had a handful of brothers to boss around and protect.

"What's up?" Miguel asked.

"Were you manning Tinker Bell?" Maverick asked him.

Miguel shook his head. "No way. That was you."

"It wasn't me," Maverick said, his voice low and awed.

"Mrs. Santos," I said.

The three of us ran to look for our teacher.

"It wasn't me. I was enjoying the show from the audience with my friends, the Burkes," she said seriously, but her eyes shone. "I think we've seen a miracle today. I do believe in fairies! I do! I do!" She clapped all the way down the hallway before she met Mrs. Burke, who sent me the warmest smile of all.

☀·☀·☀

Some things I'll never be able to explain. Like the fireflies dancing by the fairy shelter, the cupcakes, or the fairy in the last night of the show.

Other things were subtler, but even more magical. The return of my childhood, the care and love of a mother-twice-over, Mamá's happiness at being taken care of too. The thrill of adventure.

I knew Argentina wasn't an easy place. The economy was always going up and down. I watched the news and heard my mom worry about the situation there for years, after all. But my mom and the news also always agreed on one thing: Argentina was a beautiful place. Besides, things here in the US hadn't exactly been easy without a family to rely on either. In Argentina, four uncles, four aunts, and twelve cousins waited for us with open arms.

The school year was almost over in Argentina, and with the school break came summertime, Christmas, Carnaval. I was ready for the new magic. I knew the fairies would follow us everywhere because they had followed us here.

"Don't forget me," Maverick said the morning I left my mountains and everything I'd loved these past twelve years. What an adorable idiot, as if I could ever forget the first true friend of my life.

"I want to show you something," I said. I took his hand, and he followed.

Avi and Kota were leaving a goodbye present for the fairies at the fairy houses. When she saw Maverick and me, Avi gave me two thumbs up and yelled, "Minnie! YOLO!"

Maverick laughed, but his eyes sparkled, and I had to look away because I didn't want to cry. I wanted to fly.

And before I changed my mind, I hopped on the skateboard and flew down the street. The cinnamon-scented wind whipped my face. It filled me with light. I crowed like a rooster as I chased the dappled sunshine.

On the corner, I shifted my body too quickly and fell. I still hadn't mastered how to take turns, but no matter, I'd practice. I scrambled back up onto my feet. I looked behind me, and saw Maverick running along, my sisters trailing behind him, cheering me on.

I hopped back on my feet and jumped on the skateboard, and we went flying to the setting sun, all the way to the magic shores of Neverland.

Epilogue

Dear Minnie,

What's up? School isn't the same without you. Guess who got elected as the student body president for next year? None other than Jasmine, or better said, Lily, because I think after the play, that girl's possessed by the spirit of a warrior lady or something. She and her Amazons are the most popular girls in the school.

Everyone talks about you all the time. In a good way. When you come back for college, we'll make a wonderful team. Keep practicing your public speaking skills, and keep feeding those fairies. We're going to need all the fairy help we can get if we're headed to the White House to fix this mess.

Your friend who misses you,

Maverick

PS: The fairy shelter has an addition. A new family lives in your apartment, and the little girl plays outside all day, every day, even in the snow. The other night when I drove by with McKenna, it looked like there was a tiny fire. The next day, McKenna and I stopped to check. There had been no fire anywhere. But we found a mushroom fairy ring. In the winter time. I believe. I do! I do!

✷ ✷ ✷

Dear Maverick,

School here is little different, but you know how I love a challenge. In my school, they have no student body officials, but they have an honor guard for the flag, for the best scores of the year. Guess who's escorting the flag next Friday? It's the anniversary of the Malvinas Isles war, and I'm honored to hold the flag. There was a commotion with people because some complain I'm an American. I have an Argentine ID too now, and every day, just because I'm half and half, I have to prove I'm a hundred percent Argentine, and one hundred percent American. But I love the challenge! I guess I did channel a little bit of Lily, too.

Mamá . . . Mamá's doing better. Just a tiny bit, but it's been good for her to be surrounded by love. Four older brothers. Imagine that! Ha!

I see the fairies playing in the night jasmine bushes sometimes. Of course, they're dressed like hummingbirds, dragonflies, and butterflies, but I recognize them for what they are. I see them everywhere, even in Mamá's smile when Avalon talks to her in the most perfect Argentine accent.

I miss you. I'm jumping off ramps now. You better keep up your skating skills. I'm going to wow you next time I see you.

I believe. I do! I do!

The End

Acknowledgments

The process of writing this book has truly been a labor of love, years in the making. My heart spills with gratitude for the many people who have championed Minerva and her sisters (and me!) all this time.

Thank you, Stacy Whitman, for being the first person to open the doors of the publishing world to me. Winning the New Visions Award Honor for this book when it was still such a work-in-progress changed my life! None of my books would have been possible without you. Thank you for your expertise in helping me tell this story as it deserved to be told.

Thank you to the whole team at Tu Books, especially Elise McMullen-Ciotti for the expert feedback on how to portray Lily and her band of Amazon girls. Also thank you to Alethea Kontis, Sheila Smallwood, and Sarah Coleman. Bringing a book to life really takes a village!

My gratitude to Linda Camacho, my super-agent, and the whole Gallt & Zacker team knows no bounds. Thank you to Las Musas and Las Madrinas for your brilliance and friendship, especially Aída

Salazar and NoNieqa Ramos for the emotional support as I worked on this very deeply personal story. NoNi, esa velitas me ayudaron mucho!

All my love and gratitude to my fairy godmother Cynthia Leitich Smith, for believing in *Magic Shores* when it was still the bud of an idea, and to the Summer 2014 Writing and Illustrating for Young Readers (WIFYR) workshop. Thank you, Harried Plotters and VCFA. I'm so blessed to be part of so many wonderful communities, without whom I wouldn't be writing these words today: SCBWI, We Need Diverse Books, Storymakers, Latinos in Action, Kidlit Authors of Color. Librarians and teachers who share my books with readers, gracias! Thank you to the Diversity Jedi who champion representation in books and stories for all children.

To my friends: Anedia, Karina, Juli, Veeda, Courtney, Alicia, Otto, thank you!

Valynne, thanks for encouraging me to submit to the New Visions Award!

Rachel, Verónica, and Natalie: nothing would be possible without all your help. Thank you!

Endless thanks to my family in the US, Argentina, and Puerto Rico, my in-laws, cousins, tíos, and tías. Special thanks to my mom, Beatriz Aurora López, who loved fairies so much and made my childhood magical in spite of not-so-magical circumstances. Mami, te extraño todos los días de mi vida.

Julián, Magalí, Joaquín, Areli, and Valentino, I'm so honored to be your mamá!

Jeff, ¿qué te puedo decir? Gracias infinitas por tu amor y por hacerme reír todos los días.

And last but not least, gracias a mis hermanos, a quienes dedico este libro de mi corazón por la infancia tan bonita que tuvimos los cuatro juntos.

I do believe in fairies! I do, I do!

Author's Note

I'm the oldest child in my family, and even though this isn't an autobiographical story, all of Minerva's fears, dreams, and hopes were the same ones I had at her age. The preteen years are so complicated. A person can go back and forth with wanting to be a child and wanting to grow up in the space of an hour. It's an in-between place that's not comfortable for many people. It wasn't for me.

Unlike Minerva's mom, my mom never went missing, but losing her was always my greatest fear. I started writing *On These Magic Shores* shortly after she passed away, and in many ways, working through this story has helped me endure my grief. It also helped me revisit the sweetest years of my life, when my siblings and I played endlessly while she was at work.

My mother loved fairies, and as a child, *Peter Pan* was one of my favorite stories. It wasn't until I was an adult that I learned about all the flaws in the story, the racist depiction of Indians and Tiger Lily, and the limited role women and girls had in the book which has been adapted into plays and movies. But I think the story of Peter Pan has endured the passing of time because there's an undeniable appeal to remaining a child forever, especially if one is a happy child. Sadly, many children, especially children of color or those who experience financial hardship, don't even get to enjoy the childhood they do have.

In the last few years, there have been many attempts to retell the story of Peter Pan in a way that's sensitive to all people, regardless of their cultural and racial background. Since *Peter Pan* is still a favorite play for schools to show, I hope that in the future, efforts will be made to present the adapted versions that take into consideration everyone's dignity and humanity.